Praise for *Hao*

An *Electric Literature* Best Book of the Year

"Gorgeous."   —*Literary Hub*, Best Books of the Year

"Ye's writing thrives when dissecting the contradictions in life and in language."   —Javier C. Hernández,
The New York Times

"Words are Ye Chun's superpower. A translator and poet, she uses them sparsely, delicately, aware that each one carries unseen weight . . . These stories are immaculate, beautiful, tattered—like their characters."   —Hillary Kelly, *Vulture*

"Gorgeous . . . Reading Ye Chun's collection is like watching the most incredible acrobatic routine. Who knew people could do that with their bodies? Who knew someone could do that with words? . . . The women in these pages are faced with the most impossible circumstances, and they manage to make a sanctuary of words. More than anything, *Hao* is a love letter to language."   —Katie Yee, *Literary Hub*

"Poetic . . . [Ye's] characters' relentless perseverance in the face of immigration, racism and sexism comes from an inner strength as strong as the bond between mother and child."   —Katherine Ouellette, WBUR

"Ye powerfully renders the displacement felt by recent immigrants fitfully learning the language, to further highlight the cultural divide they face, and to demonstrate that they seem to have no way but forward . . . Universal and poignant."
                          —Kristen Yee, *Asian Review of Books*

"All of these sensitive tales amplify voices that have often been silenced . . . These battles are fought with pens, stick figures, tender drawings on a child's back; silent screams are in the background."   —*Kirkus Reviews* (starred review)

"Bilingual Chinese American writer, poet, and translator Ye showcases her linguistic prowess in a prodigious debut collection featuring women on both sides of the globe . . . Each of Ye's dozen stories astounds."   —*Booklist* (starred review)

"Few books capture the raw terror and exultation of motherhood, and of the implications of language itself, as gorgeously as this one. To say that *Hao* moved me doesn't feel like enough: I felt changed on the other side of these magnificent stories. *Hao* is pure triumph."   —Clare Beams, author of
                                                The Illness Lesson

"It is not often that a writer possesses the gift of rendering the missed moments of the world visible, and who finds a language for deeply meditative attention, but such is the accomplishment of Ye Chun." —Carolyn Forché, author of *What You Have Heard Is True*

"*Hao* is an unsettling, hypnotic collection spanning centuries, in which language and children act simultaneously as tethers and casting lines, the reasons and the tools for moving forward after trauma. You'll come away from this beautiful book changed." —Julia Fine, author of *The Upstairs House*

"Ye Chun captures the complexities of human emotion with a fine chisel and poet's eye, moving deftly between themes of motherhood, loss, and migration. *Hao* is a richly imagined, satisfying collection, one that invites you to stay, to linger and be moved." —Te-Ping Chen, author of *Land of Big Numbers*

"That language must be used precisely to have power feels both obvious and too often overlooked, but in Ye Chun's *Hao*, we're shown not only the continually precise and gorgeous renderings of words and phrases, but the power this can have to conjure specific ways of being, to argue against so many silent violences, and to feel like its own type of taking care. Each of these stories is an individual world brought to life fully by the particularity of its language, by Ye's extraordinarily far-reaching and deeply felt imagination, combined with her consistently stunning acuity and control."

—Lynn Steger Strong, author of *Want*

"These beautiful, profound stories are love songs to a daughter, tirades against an unjust world, and, above all, radiant meditations on Chinese history and language. Each story builds on the last with brilliance, power, and page-turning, racing energy. Surely this book will be among the best story collections of the year."   —Deb Olin Unferth, author of *Barn 8*

HAO

HAO

Stories

YE CHUN

叶春

CATAPULT

NEW YORK

Copyright © 2021 by Ye Chun

All rights reserved

Some of the stories in this collection have appeared elsewhere, in slightly different form at times: "Milk" in *The Threepenny Review* and *Pushcart Prize 2018*, "A Drawer" in *Gulf Coast*, "Wings" and "Wenchuan" in *The Bitter Oleander*, "To Say" in *Denver Quarterly*, "Crazy English" in *TriQuarterly*, "Signs" in *Conduit*, "Anchor Baby" in *Michigan Quarterly Review*, and "Hao" in *The Georgia Review* and *Pushcart Prize 2020*.

Hardcover ISBN: 978-1-64622-060-1
Paperback ISBN: 978-1-64622-155-4

Cover design by Na Kim
Book design by Wah-Ming Chang

Catapult
New York, NY
books.catapult.co

Library of Congress Control Number: 2020950765

Printed in the United States of America
1 3 5 7 9 10 8 6 4 2

For Mira

ج ج

CONTENTS

HAO

STARS

It's a swirling, crackling kind of pain, as if an electric eel is twisting inside her skull. Luyao saw such an eel in the St. Louis Aquarium during the winter break: the tank lit up every few seconds with lights powered by the eel's own voltage charges. The flashing lights had, for some reason, felt like blips of pain, and now, they are in her head, silvery, frantic. She clutches the edge of the podium and sees her students' eyes all set on her, keenly, like some high-pitched chorus. She falls silent, realizing with a sinking heart that she hasn't been making sense. She has been speaking not in English, but in Chinese, or more likely, a jumble of the two.

"I'm sorry, I'm not feeling well." She says the English words, but what comes out of her mouth sounds warped, writhing, even to her own ears. She puts a hand to her head, trying to trace the contours of the phrase "class dismissed." But as her tongue moves to its supposed position, there is nothing left to trace: the words have vanished from her brain.

Luyao does not quite remember what happens next. Only the image of the eel hunting inside her tight skull, its electricity turning words into puffs of smoke.

•

The diagnosis is a stroke. A blood clot is killing the brain cells in her left frontal lobe—specifically, the region that controls speech. Luyao, at thirty-seven, third-year doctoral student in economics, and mother of a six-year-old, has lost her ability to speak.

When her husband, Gaoyuan, arrives at the hospital, with one of his jacket collars tugged under the neckline, all she can say is one word, *hao*. The mellow-voiced doctor asks how she feels, she answers *hao*; asks her to name pictures of dogs, dolphins, and roses, she replies *hao*. *Good, yes, okay*. The most common word in Chinese, which must have been so imprinted in her memory it alone escaped the calamity. She says *hao* even when she is shaking her head and slapping her hand on the threadbare sheet of the hospital bed.

She wants to ask Gaoyuan where their daughter is. She can voice her daughter's name in her brain, Xinxin, a name she picked, meaning *happy, flourishing, thriving*, homophone to the word for *heart* and the word for *new*. "You can't find another sound with so many good meanings," she'd said to Gaoyuan. But her mouth has forgotten how to make that sound as well.

Gaoyuan does not read her mind. He's telling her what the doctor has told him. That she'd passed out, her students called 911, and an ambulance took her to the ICU. It could have been much worse. She could have lost her muscle function, or her language abilities altogether. She can still understand what others say, can still read in her head, albeit slowly.

"Xinxin is with our neighbor," he says finally. "I'll bring her tomorrow."

"Hao," Luyao says, and means it this time.

When she is alone again, encircled by a beige cubicle curtain in a corner of the hospital room, she moves all her body parts and all of them are still movable. She is lucky, they were trying to tell her. She closes her eyes and wonders if she can still cry out loud, or scream. The patient on the other side of the curtain is turning in bed, trailing long sighs with each toss. Luyao covers her ears to focus. The sound of her daughter's name. *Xinxin*. Her body quivers, her mouth fumbles, her tongue queries. But no sound except the accursed *hao* makes its way out into the air.

The next day, clinging to her father's leg, Xinxin looks at Luyao as though unsure if she is her real mother. The little girl once told Luyao where she had been before her birth: "I was so small," Xinxin said when she was around three. "I was invisible. I was sneaky, hiding from you. Then I jumped out in front of you." Luyao had felt both chill and momentary illumination. There seemed to be truth in her daughter's baby talk—this jump from being invisible to being in front of her, this will to be born and seen. If only she could think it out. But she had no time to dwell. She had been constantly busy since she went back to school, mentally absent from her daughter's logic and riddles and inventions. Only the afternoon before the stroke, Luyao stretched out an arm to stop Xinxin from climbing onto her lap: "Don't interrupt me, please. Go read a book or draw a picture."

"Mama?" Xinxin asks tentatively.

"Hao, hao." Luyao opens her arms.

·

Scott, a young speech therapist with perfectly aligned teeth, is singing "Row, Row, Row Your Boat." He asks Luyao to hum along and swings her arms with his to match the rhythm. He looks at her mouth closely as if expecting something miraculous. When he finishes the song, he moves on to "Happy Birthday." But nothing comes out of Luyao's mouth except more off-tune humming.

Scott says that it was an experiment. Rhythm and melody are controlled by the right side of the brain, which is not damaged in Luyao's case. People with her condition can sometimes blurt out the lyrics when they hum along with nursery songs. "But it probably only works for native speakers," he says.

Luyao learned those songs roughly the same time she started learning English—in middle school, in a small town in China where all her English teachers had learned their English from someone who was also Chinese. With each new teacher, Luyao inherited a different set of mispronunciations and accents, and had to unlearn and learn again. Though she was never particularly interested in English, her father had decided that she would major in the language. He predicted it would be useful, foreseeing more trade between China and English-speaking countries. He himself had majored in Russian when the two countries had called each other brothers. Luyao's pronunciations and accents continued to morph according to the professors she studied with, most of them also Chinese. She continued to learn the language perfunctorily, memorizing rules and combinations to pass exams. But in her junior year, when she was able to read unabridged literature in English, the language started to make sense to her. What seemed to be randomly arranged letters were able to generate views of far-off places she couldn't otherwise see.

After seven years of administrative work at an American pharmaceutical company in Shanghai, Luyao decided that was not what she wanted to do with the rest of her life. She applied for schools in America and got a student visa to pursue an MA in literature. She met Gaoyuan, a graduate student in math at the same East Coast university. After they graduated, neither of them could find a job, and legally they had only one year to stay. Gaoyuan applied for computer science programs and was accepted by a midwestern university. Luyao was pregnant. She moved with Gaoyuan to the college town, changed her visa from F1 to F2, and took care of the baby while applying for graduate study at the same school. This time, she too had to change majors. Business administration? Economics? Accounting? Management? Marketing? Finance? Gaoyuan made a list.

After gaining an MA in economics, Luyao was given a speaking test at the beginning of her PhD program. A computer voice asked her to open a pamphlet to page one, study a map, and give directions from a gym to a restaurant. It asked her why smoking was harmful, and what her favorite album and TV program were. Luyao had not expected to be asked such irrelevant questions and was irritated by the computer voice that kept interrupting her before she could finish. "I have no TV," she half-yelled at the computer. "Even if I had one, I wouldn't have time to watch any programs." The next day, she was informed that she had failed the test. Not only was she not allowed to teach, she had to take speaking classes.

The language instructor, Vickie, spent the next two semesters training her and other international prospective teaching assistants to speak like native speakers, which involved frequent self-recording and redoing until she and her fellow students believed that every syllable they pronounced sounded native. There was also a weekly tutorial during which Luyao sat in front of Vickie and her computer and spoke. According to Vickie, when native speakers spoke, all the words in a sentence were linked together, forming an unbroken purple line on her computer screen. "Focus," Vickie would say. "If you focus all your energy on the sound of the words, you will be able to do it." But Luyao would false-start, stumble, stutter. From time to time, she even had the paralytic feeling that she didn't know any of the words at all—they looked like alien codes, disconnected from any neurons in her brain.

Now the feeling is no longer metaphorical. As Scott

dramatically shapes his mouth around the word *hello*, the words *how are you*, and *thank you*, and *see you*, words Luyao had learned at the age of twelve, with her first English teacher who spoke English as though smacking her lips on candy—Luyao is angry.

She is angry that her father had made her major in English, when she could have majored in Chinese and in that case would never have thought of coming to study in America, where a stroke would be waiting down the road. She is angry at Gaoyuan for persuading her to switch majors. How many times when she was reading an economics textbook did she wish she were reading a novel or a book of poetry. How many sleep-deprived nights had she spent writing papers of little interest to her. She is angry at Vickie, whom she was still running into from time to time on campus and, each time, Luyao could see the words she spoke manifest themselves as broken lines on Vickie's computer screen. She'd fear that Vickie would say to her, "Let's give it another try. Let's stand here and do this till you make all the words link." Luyao is angry that during the year and a half when she was finally teaching, she couldn't help but think that her students were younger versions of Vickie, listening intently, with hidden dissatisfaction, for the unlinked words staggering out of her mouth.

Now she will never teach again, nor will she earn a PhD. She is now a disabled person who can speak no words. Except *hao*. Which is a mockery. It must have survived to tell her that she has ruined her life by saying *hao* when she should have said *bu hao*. She has compromised and strived for nothing.

.

"How was the therapy?" Gaoyuan asks at dinner.

Luyao says nothing because she doesn't want to say *hao*. He continues to look at her, so she gives him a nod.

"What words were you practicing today?" This is his final school year: he's applying for jobs and preparing for defense at the same time. Before the stroke, Luyao had been helping him edit cover letters. Their dinner conversations often had to do with the job market. Now, he doesn't talk much about it.

Luyao shakes her head, looking away.

"I learned the seasons today," Xinxin says in English.

Xinxin began speaking English to them soon after she started preschool. Luyao wanted her daughter to be a natural bilingual, an uncompromising one, able to switch between Chinese and English effortlessly, as she herself couldn't—and certainly cannot now. She had spoken to Xinxin mostly in Chinese since her birth, but a few months into preschool, Xinxin began to respond in English, asking why she needed to speak Chinese—no one else at school did. Luyao told her because it was easier to be bilingual now than later, but oftentimes, she found herself speaking English with her daughter, too tired to switch back to Chinese. She tried to make it a rule that the family would only speak Chinese at home, but more and more, she and her husband caught themselves pulled into English by their daughter, who had also started to correct their pronunciation.

"Good, what are the seasons?" Gaoyuan says in English, with a reinforced interest.

"Spring, summer, fall, winter."

"Very good. What do you know about them?"

"Spring is tornados and kind of warm. Summer is next to sunset. It looks like lots of suns. Pink is fall. Fall means leaves turn colors and the rain is kind of cold. Winter is snow. I like winter the best. No, actually I like every season the best."

"That's great, Xinxin." Gaoyuan rubs her hair.

Luyao wants to ask her daughter to repeat what she has just said. She tries to say the words in her head so that she won't forget them: *Summer is next to sunset . . . Pink is fall . . . I like every season the best.* So strange and lovely. If only she could stay inside her daughter's words and never come out.

·

In the morning, after dropping her daughter off at school, she walks to the park and sits down on a bench. A magnolia is in full bloom, its large pink flowers open deep, like sturdy throats caroling a celebratory song. A robin flits between the branches, warbling away without giving it a second thought.

Yesterday, Scott also taught her to say "My name is Luyao." His pronunciation of her name was so off it sounded like someone else's name. Still, she mimicked him. She was learning to say her own name in the wrong way.

During her first speaking class, Vickie had come in one day wrapped in a white sheet, a spiky cardboard crown on her head, a flashlight in her hand. She handed out copies of Emma Lazarus's "The New Colossus" and read it out loud. Then with more emphasis, she read again the verses containing the words "tired," "poor," "huddled masses," and "wretched refuse." "You're the 'wretched refuse' in this poem," Vickie then said to the class. "But this is a great country and we're here to help you."

Luyao had to let it go, the way she let go many of those little darts thrown her way. She had to grow thick-skinned, she told herself, and her second-class status was only temporary. In five years, she would get her PhD and become a professor. But she was too sure. She had forgotten the Eastern wisdom that the only certainty is uncertainty. Now, she has indeed become the "wretched refuse."

•

The hospital bill comes. Despite her student health insurance coverage, her portion is still five figures. She tears up the bill and throws it in the trashcan. Her and Gaoyuan's combined stipends could barely make ends meet. Now with hers gone, they won't be able to pay rent for this one-bedroom apartment, where all three of them are still co-sleeping on one mattress that covers just about the bedroom's entire floor. They will have to ask for loans from their families back in China.

She wants to go back to China. She and Gaoyuan had talked about going back many times, and the agreement was to do it if they couldn't find a job here even with a PhD. They didn't want to go back defeated, but they were nostalgic. Gaoyuan said the first thing he would do after his defense was to reread all of Jin Yong's wuxia novels. What Luyao wanted to reread was Tang poems, and she wanted to have the right mindset to read them, which she didn't foresee having anytime soon. They both knew what they were nostalgic for was not exactly the present-day China, as the country had changed so much in the last decade they could hardly keep up. Nor was it what the country had been when they lived there. But it must be there somewhere.

If it were up to her, Luyao would like to have her Chinese back. She would give away all her hard-earned English just to be able to speak like a normal Chinese again. She forms a conversation with Gaoyuan in her head:

"Can you just get a job in China so we can go back?"

"Are you sure now is a good time?"

"Yes, I'm sure. I don't want to live here another day."

"But how will living in China be different?"

"I'll try to get my Chinese back. We'll be close to our families."

"Do you really want to go back in your current condition?"

"What do you mean? Am I a disgrace now? Am I making you lose face?"

"You know that's not what I mean."

"What do you mean then?"

"I'm just being practical. What jobs do you think are available in China for people who can't speak well?"

"The same kind as here: cleaning dishes, mopping floors, wiping toilets . . ."

"Do you want to do that kind of work in China?"

"Why? Do you think people will judge me, making me a cautionary tale for those who go abroad?"

"I just don't see you doing that kind of work in China, with two master's degrees and . . ."

"That person no longer exists."

"Besides, one gets paid higher for that kind of work here than there."

"I'm not going to be your dependent, if that's what you're worried about."

To that, she can't imagine how Gaoyuan will respond. He will probably just shake his head and walk away.

Luyao has waitressed at Chinese restaurants during almost all her summer breaks and has never told any of her friends or family in China about it. It is true that no one will judge her here, as she hardly knows anyone except other Chinese graduate students who are more or less in the same boat—minus the stroke. She will ask the owner of the restaurant she's worked for the last two summers to let her do the cleaning work that even Chinese students won't do. Maybe she can bring leftover food home to save on grocery costs. Maybe she will even learn how to cook those greasy Americanized Chinese dishes. "Wretched refuse" or not, she will survive.

·

Her daughter's bedtime routine has changed. Now, Xinxin reads a book to Luyao before sleep. She points at each word and reads it out loud, modeling patiently for her to mimic, to work her lips, tongue, and vocal cords into mechanical sounds. Xinxin's favorite book is *A House Is a House for Me*, which Luyao had bought at a library sale before her stroke. She'd read it night after night to Xinxin, to the extent that one night after she finished reading, Luyao asked Xinxin to make up verses to the same effect. "What is a window a house for?" she asked.

"A window is a house for outside," Xinxin said.

"Wow, that's beautiful . . . What is outside a house for?"

"Outside is a house for future."

"Hmm, I like it. And future?"

"Future is a house for everyone."

"That's really nice. What about everyone?"

"Everyone is a house for bones."

Luyao felt her bones rattle, like those skeletons hung in

people's yards on Halloween. But her daughter's face was tranquil. The lines had all come out of her mouth without a pause, like she'd known them all along, known them intuitively. And she said the word *bones* without the least aversion, as if it was as neutral as, say, water or air.

Now, mimicking her daughter saying words from the book, Luyao thinks of Xinxin's poem again: *Future is a house for everyone. / Everyone is a house for bones.* She repeats the lines in her mind, and the paradox seems to be making a clearing in its thickets. A small clearing, but nevertheless she feels that as long as she can squeeze in and lie down there, she'll be all right for a while.

•

One night after a long day at the Chinese restaurant, about two months post-stroke, Luyao lies on the mattress with her daughter, waiting for her to fall asleep so that she can get up and finish cleaning. That's all she does now, cleaning. Her forearms shoot pain. Her knee joints feel like two handfuls of nails. The cracks on her fingers never close. Earlier, she wasn't paying attention to Xinxin's speech tutorial. She put the book away and gestured her daughter to sleep. She feels sore to the bone. Each of the bones she houses complains.

Xinxin turns in bed. Luyao can tell something is bothering her. Her daughter has not confided in her since her stroke—must have figured that her mother can offer no words of comfort anyway. Luyao pictures what could have happened to Xinxin at school. Maybe another boy walked over to her while pulling down the corner of his eyes, saying, "I'm Chinese, I can't see." Or another girl told her she couldn't be her friend anymore because she didn't believe in God and would go to hell. Or the girl who told Xinxin that the Easter Bunny didn't bring her anything because he didn't recognize her as an American said another damaging thing. Back then, Luyao was able to tell Xinxin that those children were ignorant, that she was born here. She is an American just like any other child.

Now Luyao has about thirty words she can form with her mouth. She still has no spontaneous sentences. She draws Xinxin to her arms and kisses her head. Xinxin sighs, and then starts to sing a lullaby. It is the lullaby Luyao had made up for her when she was a newborn. It's in Chinese. A simple melody with lyrics all about something or someone falling sleep, starting with the stars, then the moon, the trees, the birds, or the streets, the streetlamps, and after every seven lines is the refrain "Xinxin ye yao shui jiao le"—Xinxin is also falling asleep.

Now Xinxin is singing it, improvising, inserting Chinese nouns she knows in the lyrics. Then, she stops. In the quiet, Luyao hears her own voice, clear and supple like water, singing the refrain, "Xinxin ye yao shui jiao le." Unable to believe it's true, she sings it again. For the first time since her stroke, she is able to say a sentence, and her daughter's name, effortlessly.

Luyao and Xinxin are both laughing when Gaoyuan appears at the door. Luyao sings it to him.

"Hao, hao, tai hao le," Gaoyuan says.

Luyao says *hao* too, and for the first time, it seems, she feels the immense goodness in this word.

•

Later that night, after her daughter falls asleep, Luyao cleans the kitchen and takes the trash out of the apartment to the dumpster. On her walk back, she counts seven stars above her head. She knows there are countless others up there, only that the night is not dark enough to reveal them. Like the words in her mind, they are there somewhere, none missing. She keeps her face raised and says *Xinxin ye yao shui jiao le* to the seven stars.

She looks around the sky and sees more. With care, she

says the words she has relearned so far one by one. She says each word quietly, slowly, as if dedicating them to each of the stars. *Hello. Thank you. See you.* More stars emerge from the infinity.

GOLD MOUNTAIN

1870s

Ah Lian can almost pretend she is back in the Middle Kingdom, as here in San Francisco Chinatown, Chinese are just about all she sees, except that they are all men—clothed either like her husband in dark satin changshans, or in coarse cotton shirts. They linger at a store or saunter down the street, as she peeks out of her second-story window. She has gone outside the apartment with her husband only once—during the Spring Festival celebration a few weeks after her arrival, and the men stared at her instead of the dancing dragon, as though she was the spectacle, standing there in her silk blouse that turned transparent in their eyes.

Her husband has not taken her out since. From his store downstairs, he brings up groceries that she cooks and serves. He brings red bean and mung bean pastries that look just like the ones at home but taste different somehow, staler, and with a hint of a foreign smell that does not belong to the food category. It is the smell of the ship, a mixture of salt, unclean sweat, and human waste. The ever-present odor of her monthlong journey reaches her again.

He also brings a zheng home that he finds at the pawn shop down the street. "A wonder to see something like this here," he says.

He asks her to learn to play. She has never touched an instrument before. She has actually only seen a zheng played once back home, by a blind woman in the market for money, its music like thousands of little bells ringing in succession. Ah Lian keeps her fingernails long and tries different combinations of strings. The sounds she makes are not bell-like but remind her of the bamboos' shushing behind her old house. Her father and grandfather are both bamboo furniture makers. She used to make bamboo baskets and bowls with her mother and sisters. She never imagined she would miss those green plants growing tall and mindless to the sky. They were as common as dirt then.

At night after dinner, her husband asks her to play

while he sips tea. He is her father's age but gentler than her father. She plays and hears wind rushing through bamboos, their hollow stems knocking and echoing, their lance-shaped leaves flipping and cutting the air. Her husband steps over and kisses her neck slowly. "Keep playing," he whispers in her ear. She picks, plucks, pushes, and pulls the strings until with her half-closed eyes she sees silver dots like those cast by the sun on the deep grove.

In the morning, she finds ways to follow the sun, which comes in through the front window. She cannot be too close to the window, as men living on the block know she is here and have the habit of looking up to catch a glimpse of her. Are they all dreaming of her at night? Please your husband, do whatever he wants on the wedding night, her mother advised her. Her mother, of course, referred to the night when Ah Lian finally got to meet her husband in Gold Mountain. There wasn't a real wedding or wedding night. In the brief ceremony back across the ocean, she knelt beside a rooster she had to hold down when it struggled to flap away. She slept alone in a small moldy room in her husband's old house where his parents, first wife, and two grownup children lived—for one night, before she was escorted to Hong Kong to depart for Gold Mountain.

Ah Lian was not so naïve as to think that Gold Mountain would be a mountain covered by gold. Just as she knows that the Pearl River is not a river flowing with pearls. But still, she was surprised by how little gold there was to see. As her husband drove her in a rented buggy uphill from the wharf to Chinatown, the only golden-looking thing was the hair of several white men pelting stones at a column of Chinese laborers who had just disembarked from the same ship—now dodging clumsily while carrying all their belongings on bamboo poles.

Her husband took her without giving her time for a bath. She had longed for a real bath, after all she'd got for the past month were rushed washings from buckets of rainwater. When he took her, she could still smell the ship in her pores. She was still in the motion of the tumbling sea. She feared if she didn't please him, he would send her back. She would give anything not to get on that ship again. She'd seen a girl climb up the railing and jump into the ocean, which swallowed her in one gulp, and another, whose berth was right by Ah Lian's, dead with her face covered in vomit.

•

Soon Ah Lian's husband also brings bags of shrimps for her to peel and can. They are to be sold in his grocery store downstairs. Her fingers turn soggy. When she plays the zheng, the raw smell seems to be coming out of her own body.

An older wife who lives a couple blocks away, whose husband runs a hardware store, comes to visit her one day. She tells her about another new wife who got the idea of taking a walk by herself. Guess what happened? Some devils grabbed her hair and dragged her back and forth on the street. Another wife got her apartment broken into after her husband died and two kidnappers spirited her away to the mountains. What for? What do you think? Sold her to a brothel in one of the mining towns snowbound all year round.

Ah Lian has a daughter ten months later. A midwife comes and goes. Ah Lian lies in bed, nursing her baby and falling in and out of sleep, the same ocean rhythm: as though she is back in the hold of the ship, except that there are no other passengers beside her and her infant, and the ship will not reach the shore. All the men passing below the window are sea creatures not to mingle with. They will swallow her alive if they get hold of her. Her husband is a shipmate who comes to check if she is still alive. She will pretend she is when he makes love to her at night. Do what he pleases, as she was advised.

She is here to stay, after all, now for the second year, her daughter three months old. What else does she expect?

She doesn't want to be the second wife, but she doesn't have to wait in an empty bedroom for the rest of her life like the first wife, nor does she need to serve the parents-in-law. What's there to complain about? She watches her baby's hair sprout. Sometimes when she opens her eyes from a slumber, her baby will be looking at her, eyes steady, as if to read her fortune.

Sometimes, with the baby strapped to her chest, Ah Lian plucks the strings of the zheng. She closes her eyes the way the blind woman in the market did and plays while picturing things she hasn't seen since she left home, such as her mother's and sisters' faces as they sat together weaving strips of bamboo into baskets, such as the egg flowers they picked and let dry in the sun for soup, or the fabric shops they loitered around on market days.

She goes out of the apartment with her husband one more time to attend someone's baby son's full-moon cele-bration. On their way back from the clan association, her husband carries their baby girl and walks steps ahead of Ah Lian, leaving her struggling to keep up on her small feet. A group of white boys appear on the other side of the street and start to throw things at her. Something hits. She touches the side of her neatly arranged bun: it's a rotten egg. They laugh, mimicking the way she walks, and cover their noses to show she stinks. Her husband turns to yell at them in English. The white boys parrot his angry words as if to throw them right back at him. He retraces a few steps and grabs Ah Lian's arm. "Quick," he says between his teeth. "Can't you even walk?"

•

She is pregnant again and cannot stand the smell of shrimp, so her husband brings cigar parts for her to roll. From time to time, he still asks her to play zheng after dinner, but she'll tell him she is not feeling well. Besides, she says, she has to cut her nails to roll the cigars.

Two white ladies come to visit once. Ah Lian's husband leads them up the stairs as they tell him they're making a round of visits to all merchant wives in Chinatown. They wear tight tops that push up their breasts. The older lady speaks Cantonese that she'd learned during her years of missionary work in Canton. The younger one seems to be holding her breath. They show Ah Lian a picture of their God with his golden hair and golden halo. And pictures of rooms with large windows and flower vases. "Look," the older lady points at the wallpaper on each of the pictures. "It's nice to have this on the wall. A clean house will evoke God's presence." The younger lady is trying not to cast too many glances at the altar of Guanyu, where a bowl of rice and cups of tea and wine are placed on the shelf, or the smaller altar of Guanyin where Ah Lian prays for a baby son, or at Ah Lian's feet.

When Ah Lian is seven months pregnant with the new baby, San Francisco has a smallpox outbreak. The city government orders all houses in Chinatown fumigated. "They blame us for everything," her husband says. "Even though they're the ones who drink unboiled water and hardly ever wash themselves. That stink of theirs—"

There're only enough bottles and tin jars to seal half of the produce in the store. They save as much as they can in a cart, which Ah Lian's husband pushes out of Chinatown. She walks by him, holding their toddler daughter by the hand, to the park nearby. Ah Lian stands with a dozen or so wives and their children, encircled by their husbands. Away from them stand another group of women, larger in number—the One Hundred Men's Wives. They are guarded by brothel keepers in black tunics and brimmed hats. The two groups of women steal glances at each other as they chat among themselves, until the western sky is suddenly lit with streaks of blood and orange. Ah Lian's daughter points at the sun, a booming orb more golden than anything Ah Lian has ever seen. That's *taiyang*, she says, realizing she hasn't seen a sunset since she got off the ship.

Her second baby is again a girl. Her husband brings more piecework for her to do. He goes out after dinner, leaving the store to his hired hand for all the evening hours. He comes back late, his breath reeking of liquor.

Sometimes while he is away, Ah Lian straps the newborn to her chest and plays zheng. "That's the sound of bamboos," she tells her daughter. She tries to describe what bamboos look like, how it feels to be standing in the middle of their tall stems, how the world seems to be nothing else, just that green and wind. She can't quite find the words, so she plays. Her daughter will fall asleep on the cushion beside her.

·

One early evening, putting her children to bed, Ah Lian hears noises out on the street. Lifting a corner of the curtain, she sees men running, peddlers stuffing their wares into baskets, store tenders hurling goods inside and shutting doors. The stairs creak beneath her as their hired hand yells up, "Madam, keep your door locked. Dim the lights. The devils are coming! Hundreds of them!"

"My husband?"

"Haven't seen him. Must be in one of the dens. I have to go."

She hears the store door downstairs screech shut, the chain lock clink. She checks the latch of the apartment door, and as she blows out the oil lamps one by one, she hears a gunshot. Her baby bawls. Her daughter crawls underneath the bed. In the dark, Ah Lian fumbles back to the living room and, adjusting her eyes, pushes the table in front of the door. She returns to the bedroom, picks up her baby from the bed, and then bends down to reach for her daughter.

They huddle on the floor between the wall and the bed. She hears more gunshots, and with each of her heartbeats, shouting and stomping come closer. There must be an army of them, marching, yelling something over and over in unison. The floor shakes, the windowpanes shudder. Reflections of torch lights roll across the curtain. She hears bangs and kicks on the front door downstairs. The smash of wood and glass. She holds her children tight, whispering "hush" in their ears.

As the looting goes on below them, women's screams from somewhere down the street cut through the clamor. She covers her children's ears and shuts her eyes. She imagines flying. Holding one child in each arm, she will fly across the ocean and land inside the bamboo grove behind her old house. The dense, tall stems will receive them, closing up around them without a trace.

The looting lasts most of the night. In the early morning, when both the street and downstairs grow quiet, Ah Lian carries her sleeping children to the bed and tiptoes to the door. She listens, and just as she's pondering whether to push the table away to take a peep, she hears men talking in English again. Are they here to scavenge what's left from the loot? Or have they occupied the store, just waking up from their sleep?

She tiptoes to the kitchen and picks up a cutting knife from the counter. There's hardly any food left in the apartment: her husband has always been the one bringing groceries up as needed. Where is he now? She sees him, half-drunk, dragged onto the street and trampled by every booted foot of every shouting man. She shakes her head to rid it of the image. Still clutching the knife, she tiptoes back to the living room and kneels down in front of the altars. In the gray, smoky air filtering in through the curtain, the statuette of Guanyin looks small, flimsy. Guanyu's red, fiery face looks like a grimace.

Chinatown awakes with white men's yelling all over again. Even though the shouts are no longer in unison, the righteousness and festivity linger in them. There are also the sounds of whips and horse trots as loads of loot are carted off. At her children's first sniffle, Ah Lian puts down the knife and huddles them again into her arms. She waits till the downstairs is quiet, and then straps her baby to her chest. With her daughter hanging on to her leg, she removes the small bowl of rice from the Guanyu altar and boils it in a pot of water.

It's not until the next morning when she comes to the door again. She pushes away the table and unlatches the door. She has listened for most of the night to the devils doing their devilish things. She has peeked from behind the curtain in the first blue and seen her countrymen step out of their hiding places, their backs bent, their cotton-soled shoes light on the dirt street. Holding the knife in one hand, she opens the door. The sight of what's left of the store shocks her, but she does not avert her eyes. As she walks down the steps, she feels as if she is climbing down a mountain, which is not made of gold, but of dust, shards, and all the broken, ravaged things.

HAO

1966

Qingxin remembers that the character 万 comes from 𝔜 in the Oracle Bone Script—a scorpion with large pincers and a poisonous stinger at the end of its jointed tail. How does a bug come to mean *ten thousand*, as in "毛主席万岁"—*May Chairman Mao live ten thousand years*, a slogan she's made to write a thousand times a day? She wants to look it up in 《说文解字》, her classical dictionary, but all her books were confiscated and burned. If she remembers correctly, it's speculated that scorpions once plagued the Central Plain, so when people saw the sign, they saw not just one scorpion but tens of thousands of them. Now, three millennia later, on the same Central

Plain, she is labeled "毒蝎"—*poisonous scorpion*, and ordered to write a word that comes from the same insect a thousand times a day. Is she, then, a poisonous scorpion, releasing tens of thousands of scorpions back to the Central Plain each time she writes down the word?

Another label she's given is "牛鬼蛇神"—*ox demon serpent god*. Back before the Revolution, these gods and demons with human bodies and animal heads had powers and were treated with reverence. Now people labeled so are shaved a Yin-Yang Head and made to kneel, their faces distorted in fear and shame and in their effort to endure something they don't know they can endure. Their bodies remain human bodies that bleed and break easily while subject to hours of beating by their former students, who are given a new name too—Red Guards. What are they guarding? Their human sun, the Chairman? Sometimes Qingxin wonders if Chairman Mao is indeed a god and will indeed live ten thousand years as she is condemned to write a thousand times a day.

"If you look at history," her husband would say, "Qinshihuang did the same thing—*burn books and bury scholars*—so that nothing except his own words would count. There're only minor differences: one called himself the First Emperor, the other Chairman; one had scholars buried alive, the other has them tortured day after day by the students-turned-killers. You can tell those little monsters are enjoying it. They'll eat us if they're asked to. This is not a world to live in. We'll soon lose the last bit of dignity."

In the dark bed of their old apartment he would say those things, and she would hush him with "People can hear you," looking around their small room as though ears were concealed in the lightless air. Their four-year-old daughter slept between them, her breaths faintly audible, each a thin hook cast into the unknown.

·

The character 无 is simplified from 無, which comes from 𣉥—a person dancing, waving bouquets of flowers, for the dead. Now, the word means *zero, nothing*. There's no more dancing for the dead, no rituals, just a dead body dumped somewhere, turned into zero. His body was dragged onto the shore. Three Red Guards took her there: "We got something to show you." They looked mischievous. There was no dignity in that waxen face either, with garbage caught in his collar, riverweed in his hair.

They told her to slap his face. She looked at them.

"Slap his face—he is bad," one said. "He knew he was bad. That's why he killed himself, which makes him even worse."

"There's no need to explain to her," another said. "You do what we tell you to do. You are all bad!"

Both had been in her Chinese class and her husband's history class—that was two months ago, in the pre-revolutionary era, when they were merely adolescent bullies with military fathers. Now they are judges and executioners.

His skin felt damp, rubbery. Since the Cultural Revolution started, she had not really touched his face—it would have been too much to bear that gesture of sympathy, of looking into each other's eyes and saying, "We will be fine. We will survive this." She couldn't make herself put on such an act, and she knew neither of them would want to receive it.

"Slap him! Not stroke!" they yelled, then laughed.

•

Now, when her daughter, Ming, asks about her father, Qingxin tells her he has gone to a place where he can sleep. "He hasn't been able to sleep much," she says. "Now he can sleep without ever being bothered again."

Ming is quiet for a while. Then she says, "Word game, Mama. Let's play our word game."

It's their bedtime ritual. A game Qingxin devised when Ming turned four—months before the Revolution, before their world was flipped upside down—figuring it was time to teach her how to write. So instead of giving her the routine backrub, she started to write words on her back. Oftentimes, Qingxin picks words that are pictographic, their origins traceable to the Oracle Bone Script, the beginning of Chinese written language's bloodline. She will start with a word's original form and let Ming guess what it is, and then trace its evolution to its current simplified version. Which was how she used to teach her students—when they were still students—so that they knew words were not made of random strokes, that each came into being for a reason, with logic behind it, and thoughts and imagination.

Now logic fails. Thoughts and imagination are reserved for cruelty and survival. But more than ever, Ming has been insisting on playing the word game every night.

"Mama is tired. Go to sleep now."

But she fusses, cries. "Word game, Mama. Let's play our word game."

"Not today. Go to sleep."

Ming cries louder, turning her back against her, her little shoulders shuddering. Qingxin holds her in her arms and cries with her. A few minutes later, Ming starts again, "Our word game, Mama. Write my name and your name."

Slowly, Qingxin writes her daughter's name, 明, an

ideogram that hasn't changed much since its origin, a compound combining the two pictograms 日 and 月, *sun* and *moon*, meaning *bright*. A word Qingxin picked, and since the Revolution, she has wondered if she'd had the prescience of the dark age falling. More than any time now, her daughter needs a name like this to keep her out of darkness's way. But how will things be bright for her both in daytime and at night? What a grand and impossible hope it now seems.

Qingxin's own name is even more impossible: 清心, *clear-water heart*, or *heart like clear water*. "When our heart is quiet and clear," her mother, who practiced Chan, told her, "we don't feel pain. We want no more, no less, just this moment as we breathe." Both Qingxin's mother and father were classified "Rightists" and sent away to separate prisons in separate provinces. Qingxin doesn't know if they're alive or dead, or if their minds are set free—or if they are able to think of the name they gave her and breathe and feel no pain.

•

In the mornings, Qingxin does janitorial work, cleaning the school compound and toilets. In the afternoons, she's taken to the town square for the struggle session, made to kneel with a cardboard sign hanging around her neck, with three lines of words: "牛鬼蛇神 / 坏 / 余清心"—*ox demon serpent god / bad / Yu Qingxin*—and an X across each character of her name. Yelled at, kicked, and beaten, she keeps her head down. After the session, the Red Guards take her back to the school, into one of the former classrooms, which are now called "牛棚"—*cowsheds*, to copy the slogan "毛主席万岁" a thousand times—a way, as they put it, to "atone" for her husband's suicide. Gripped by the new pains from the new beating, she sits in front of a desk, completes this "assignment" in a student notebook.

One day, about a week into this daily copying, she raises her head from the notebook and sees her blunder: instead of the word "万"—*ten thousand*, she has been writing "无"—*nothing, zero*—that is, instead of *May Chairman Mao live ten thousand years*, she has been writing *May Chairman Mao live zero years*. Not once or twice, one page or two, but for four pages, several hundred times, she has replaced the word.

She is alone in the "cowshed," but they are coming. It's close to the time they come to collect her "homework," give her a final scolding or beating, and then, if all goes well, let her leave to pick up her daughter. She will need to tear the four pages off and make them disappear quickly. But the room is locked. She cannot go to the bathroom and flush the pages down the toilet. She cannot shred the pages with her fingers and throw them into the dustbin or hide them in her clothes. The guards will see the tear, will search for the shreds, find them, and patch them up.

She's shoving the last handful of paper into her mouth when the door unlocks. A Red Guard, a slender girl with darting eyes, steps in—also a former student of hers, a good, respectful one exceling in composition and handwriting, who now keeps her face stoic and avoids eye contact.

"What—what are you chewing?" Her expression is a mix of alarm and annoyance, as though she's convinced that her former teacher—now an "ox demon"—is taunting her with a new kind of perversity: chewing paper like an ox chomping grass. Gluey pulps form in the corners of her mouth.

Qingxin cannot answer. All she can do is shake her head and try to swallow the dry, half-chewed paper as quickly as possible.

The girl looks at the door, but the other Red Guards are not coming yet: she has to deal with this alone. Her face hardens. She walks over and picks up the notebook. Despite Qingxin's attempt to remove the torn edges from the seam, the girl notices the tear right away. She narrows her eyes at it, then flips through the remaining pages.

"You didn't finish today's assignment," she says, her

eyes still on the pages that are covered with the same five words, like the same insects crawling, gathering, multiplying. "Why are you eating pages from the notebook?"

Qingxin makes a difficult final swallow. "I didn't like the handwriting on those pages. I only want to write those sacred words in the best handwriting possible"—saying what she prepared to say.

"I don't believe you. There's no need to eat bad handwriting. Why don't you just tell me the truth?"

"That is the truth." And again Qingxin sees her daughter waiting on the front porch of her preschool, always one of the last to be picked up—small on the top of the darkening stairs, leaning toward the direction where her mother must eventually appear. "Please believe me. I don't like bad handwriting. You know me—"

"Don't talk to me like that. I don't know you. You're not my teacher anymore. You're the class enemy. Don't forget that."

"I know, I know. Please let me redo them. I'll finish this in no time."

The girl considers, her face turning malleable, and for a moment the room seems to pulsate with the possibility of decency. But they both hear something: their eyes turn to the door—the three other Red Guards are rushing in, those who dragged Qingxin to the riverbank.

"What's going on?" they yell.

And instantly, the girl's posture changes to alert. "She lied to me," she says without looking at her. "She wrote something bad in the notebook. She was eating up the pages when I came in."

·

At some point during the beating, Qingxin stops feeling any pain. Even the thought of her daughter leaves her. Her mind must have risen up quietly as though not to disturb the scene or not to continue witnessing it. Her mind flies away from the room, the school building, alights on a tree, a bird. But after circling over the city, maybe for ten minutes or an hour, it eventually flies back to her daughter, who is now sitting on a little stool inside the school, her gaze on the front door. Near her, the hunchback janitor is mopping the floor, grumbling about his own share of misery in this torturous world.

·

Because of her new crime, Qingxin is no longer allowed to live in her apartment. She and her daughter are put in a closet-size storeroom in the school. It is windowless and smells of mildew, a third of its space occupied by brooms, mops, and buckets that Qingxin uses for the janitorial work. She folds a blanket to the size of the remaining surface and spreads it on the floor.

After Qingxin switches off the one light bulb above their heads, Ming says the words Qingxin knew were coming: "Word game, Mama. Let's play our word game."

Despite this knowing, the word *word* makes her shudder. She can taste again the inky paper: bitter, like bugs jammed into her mouth. What could have gotten into her to replace 万 with 无, a word that comes from scorpion to a word that meant, once upon a time, dancing for the dead? Did she, deep in her consciousness, need to dance for her dead husband, instead of adding more poisonous scorpions to this plagued land? Or, did she covertly wish Chairman Mao would turn into nothing, zero, instead of living ten thousand years—a wish so powerful it bled through her fingers that held the pen, through the ink onto the paper of the notebook?

"No more word games. We're not playing that game again."

"But Mama, we do it every night."

Ming cries. Qingxin lets her. But word game or not, there is no way to know what's coming next—no way to know that another "crime" will not befall her, nor that she will survive another beating. There is simply no way. Which is why people end their lives, by whatever means available—drowning in the river, leaping off a building, hanging from a tree or a ceiling, swallowing sleeping pills or insecticide, cutting their throats open with a pair of scissors or stabbing their hearts with a kitchen knife—so they do not have to not know.

Qingxin has a pillow. She can wait until her daughter falls asleep and put it on her small breathing face to make the sleep permanent. Then it will just be herself, and she will be easy to finish.

She holds her daughter in her arms and moves her hand across her small back, which feels soft and alive, as though all that is tender and good in the world is condensed in there. Ming's cries gradually subside to intermittent sobs, and then, when Qingxin thinks she has fallen asleep, Ming suddenly asks in the dark, in a quiet, measured voice that does not quite belong to a four-year-old, "Mama, are you going to die?"

The tears that Qingxin has been holding back slide down her cheeks. She tries to keep her voice even: "Yes, someday. Everyone dies. But I won't die until I know you are safe."

"How are you not going to die?" Ming asks, turning to lie on her back and gaze at the dark ceiling.

"I will—I will take good care of you and take good care of myself."

Ming turns her face back to her mother and nestles her head on her chest.

And then, with a little finger, she starts to draw on Qingxin's skin, just below her collarbone, her own name, 明, a sun and a moon. With each stroke, each touch, Qingxin feels a trickle of coolness, an easing, flowing. Her pain begins to loosen its fists and knots. Her body feels lighter, as if light is receiving her, and she and her daughter are not here in the windowless storeroom, but outside, on a green meadow where moonlight hums.

Then Ming draws Qingxin's name, 清心, clear-water heart. The two words her parents named her. On the cardboard she wears in front of her chest, the words are crossed out, as though that person no longer exists and in her place is this reduced half-human-half-animal that can no longer own the name. But her daughter is writing it on her bare skin right now, stroke by stroke. And somewhere in her vision, Qingxin sees a body of clear water that is also inside her own body—which is her parents' wish for her, to be able to return there, to go back to her breath and know that she can be as calm and clean as water that knows no pain, nor resistance or fear.

·

The moment when she survives another beating becomes expansive. She will not show her amazement after knowing that she is still alive, still able to move her arms and legs and breathe without too much pain. Still allowed to go see her daughter. To be able to do all that for another day surprises her, as though she does not know her own dimension, or how far her life can be stretched without snapping. She is relearning how to live this life. Already she has learned to better endure the beating—stay still or twist the body in a way to protect the head. And to be only partially there when they humiliate her: those shaming songs they make her sing, she sings without letting the words sink in; those self-condemning words they force her to say, she says without letting them cling.

She is able to believe none of those words matter when she lets her finger move across her daughter's back and draws the real words on her skin—words scripted with love, free from malice. Usually, they're simple words about the natural elements—star, wind, mountain, river, the seasons, the colors, types of animals, names of plants and flowers. As though she's recreating the world, its blue hills, clouds like pagodas, blooming trees, laughing children, pairs of wings.

As Qingxin endures the day, she thinks of a word to give her daughter at night, like a gift, a talisman, to take care of her and take care of herself. An amulet to save them from harm and keep them alive for another day.

One night, she draws on her daughter's back the word for fountain, 泉, which comes from 泉 —water flowing out of a mountain cave. She describes the mountain. How quiet it is: you can hear each birdcall and its echo between the rock faces and the sound of water gurgling just out of view. The two of them have climbed along the stony path toward the fountain. "Now we're here," she says. "Let's drink." She cups her palms into a bowl; her daughter does the same. They reach over, feel the cool water touching their skin, filling them up, and quickly they hold the water to their lips. "Ah," they say, "how cool, how sweet." Ming giggles. She does too.

But then she is afraid. She holds her daughter tightly in her arms, doesn't know if she is doing the right thing—to make her believe there can be joy in this world that does not tolerate joy, not even from a four-year-old. Those people will not tolerate seeing them smile, seeing the sun on their faces. They will want to crush that, too.

•

Some nights she cannot lift her finger. "Our word game," her daughter will say. "Let's play our word game." But Qingxin does not want to make the effort or feel those decent human feelings. They seem too fine, too contradictory to the rest of her existence. Too incoherent, false, fake. But her daughter will insist, "Draw words, Mama. Draw my name and your name," and will touch her face with her hand.

"Mama is tired. You draw on me."

And Ming will start to draw—on Qingxin's chest, her palm, a piece of skin that is not cut or bruised—her name: a sun and a moon; her mother's name: clear-water heart. Qingxin thinks, *May the sunlight and moonlight shine on her path so that she will not get lost; may my mind be as clear and calm as water.*

Then she will hold her daughter, and it is as if the holding turns her into a lake—no longer hard and clenched, but liquid. Then she will start drawing a new word on her daughter's back.

•

She is thinking of words that do not signify the natural elements, the rudimental, everlasting things that will outlive this upturned world. The word 好, for example, the opposite of the word 坏 that is on the cardboard she carries every day. The most common word in Chinese, a ubiquitous syllable people utter and hear all the time, which is supposed to mean *good*. But what is *hao* in this world, where good books are burned, good people condemned, meanness considered a good trait, violence good conduct? People say *hao* when their eyes are marred with suspicion and dread. They say *hao* when they are tattered inside.

But she thinks of the word itself. It comes from 好, a kneeling person with breasts, a woman, 女, holding a child, 子. It suits her, doesn't it? At night she holds her daughter in her arms, and in the daytime, as she is made to kneel in front of others, she is still holding her, even though no one sees it.

And she thinks again of the word 坏 that hangs in front of her chest and is yelled into her face every day, which comes from 壞, a person crying by the crumbled city wall for her lost home. It also suits her in that sense: she is the one who has lost her husband, her home, and wants to cry by the crumbled world.

She thinks of each word as a seed, an origin, a center where its meanings radiate. Then, when she draws a word on her daughter's back, that clean slate, that virgin land, she will be able to imagine she is writing it for the first time. She is planting a seed, and together they will name it, nurture it, give it new meanings, and salvage it from hate and abuse.

.

So, in the narrow room with no light, she draws a sun and a moon on her daughter's back. She draws a lake of clear water and a heart. And then, she draws a kneeling person with breasts.

"Why is she kneeling?" Ming asks.

"Why do you think?"

"Because she is tired?"

"Yes, she is tired," Qingxin says, "but not too tired to hold her child." She draws a child by the woman.

"That's us: you holding me."

"Yes, that's us." And she lets her hand rest on her daughter's soft, unscarred back.

ANCHOR BABY

"Actually, there's something I want to ask you," he says after bringing the groceries to the living room. "Have you heard of the term *anchor baby*? *Anchor*. Do you know what it means?"

She can't interpret that look of his, nor the tone of his voice. He may suddenly burst into laughter and say something like *Look at your face; I'm joking*. That seems to be the logical conclusion to such a question, which she senses is meant to insult, as it is unfathomable for a man who has been polite to her to suddenly talk like that. This is the second time he helped her carry groceries upstairs. He also knocked on her door once, telling her she'd left her key in the lock.

He shakes his head, his face settling into a semi-grin, like he is recognizing something deeply ironic in the situation. He sits down on the couch without being asked to, his eyes now level with her belly, which is in her thirty-eighth week of pregnancy, fourteen days before she's due.

She has only vaguely heard of the term before, maybe in the articles she read on the internet while preparing to come here—about raids on the West Coast where this kind of birth service is more developed but also more prone to disasters: women with bursting bellies or suckling newborns taken to police stations for visa fraud or money laundering. Mrs. Liang told her that she was not running a business—she was merely renting out her condo and providing pregnancy and postpartum assistance to her, which was perfectly legal. And what you're doing—coming here on a tourist visa and giving birth to a child—is perfectly legal too. Just relax and enjoy the rest of your pregnancy and bring home a U.S.-citizen baby, she told her after picking her up at the airport, before leaving her alone in this small condo, which was described as "spacious and luxurious" in the ad and had indeed looked so in the photos.

Now the man sits in the living room that she has decked up a little with a vase of lilies, a bamboo plant, and a few stuffed animals for the baby. He looks at her with a glint in his eyes, as if he's stimulated by the fact that he has said what he said, and that now there is nothing to stop him from saying more. Or as if he is equally curious to see how she will respond and what he will do next.

But she has not let the term stick. It doesn't matter what they will call her baby. All that matters is that she will be born a U.S. citizen, not a bastard, as she would have been if she were born in China. But you can go to Hong Kong or Singapore, Lao Li had said. Why does it have to be America? Because, she'd said, I only want the best for our child.

The man is about Lao Li's age, tall, skinny, with big feet; his floor creaks in the evenings when he moves about in the upstairs condo. Fleetingly, she has imagined what he might be like in bed, how he would be different from Lao Li—as she lay alone, among IKEA furniture you see often in China, her body expansive, her skin aglow, with nothing but her own hands to quell her hunger. Besides hunger, there has been a vague trepidation that lurks in the back of her head, the pit of her stomach. Only a couple nights ago, she dreamt of a chicken claw sticking out of her belly, the rest of the chick, or baby, about to spill out.

"I don't know," she says to the man. She must feign ignorance, pretend nothing wrong is going on. Intuition tells her she must not confront. She must look as if she doesn't get it. She is a foreigner, a Chinese—the cultural gap makes his words and behaviors untranslatable.

"I'll look it up for you. You know how to read English, right?" He takes out his cell phone from his pants pocket and starts scrolling and typing on the screen.

She had taken mandatory English from middle school through college, and after finding out she was pregnant, she enrolled at an adult education center to refresh her language skills. If her baby's future is in America, her future will be here too. At least that was what she thought then.

"Why?" she says. "Why do you ask me about this?"

He ignores her question, holding up his cell phone for her to see. "This is what *anchor* means. Take a look."

She reads the first definition:

> *anchor*
> *—noun*
> *1. any of various devices dropped by a chain, cable, or rope to the bottom of a body of water for preventing or restricting the motion of a vessel or other floating object, typically having broad, hook-like arms that bury themselves in the bottom to provide a firm hold.*

Her daughter, who grows bigger in her belly every day, does not have "broad, hook-like arms." On the sonogram, they look rather short and thin, more like fish fins that help her float than metal arms that "provide a firm hold."

"Why?" she asks again. "Why do you ask?"

"Isn't the baby you're carrying going to be an anchor baby? No offense, but am I wrong?"

If her baby who is due in fourteen days is an anchor, then she is a boat. She does feel like a boat with full-winded sails sometimes, ample, unmoored, navigating unknown waters. Why did she decide to sail all the way and drop her anchor here? To give her child the best. But now America is this real place, just like Lao Li, who used to stand for something—maturity, wealth, confidence, success—all the things that she did not have herself, in the end was revealed to be this real, aged person with large pores and a quick temper. The man sitting in front of her was also an idea before—a well-mannered gentleman who helped her with groceries and told her she'd forgotten her key—but has now suddenly turned real, sinister.

"I don't know what you mean. I need to cook dinner. I'm eating for two, you know." She tries to smile, to be amiable. There is the saying *yi rou ke gang*, to conquer the hard with the soft. That is what she's got—the soft and yielding, which may appear to be a weakness, but she draws power from it. She has done that with Lao Li, never confronting him, giving him what he wants, in exchange for what she wants. What did she want then? A condo, a savings account, a monthly allowance, an easier life than the working one in which you start as an assistant and climb and climb, not ever able to save enough and buy a one-bedroom. At least she knows what Lao Li wants. What does this man want?

He remains seated, looking at her as though she has said nothing. She glances at the door, which is partially closed. Two people are talking and walking down the stairs—her next-door neighbors, who make either tumultuous love or loud arguments across the wall. If she yells now, they may still be able to hear her.

"That Chinese lady who comes here from time to time. Are you related to her?"

Maybe he is secret police, here to arrest her. And before he does it, showing all his cards, he will torment her first.

"Yes, she is my aunt." To visit my aunt in Maryland, she had told the customs officer when asked the purpose of her visit. Mrs. Liang lives in a house in the suburbs with her postman husband and three children and is always busy. She will chat with her during the car ride to and from the doctor's office and drop her off outside the condo despite an invitation to come up and have some tea. According to their agreement, Mrs. Liang will *zuo yuezi* for her after the baby is born, sleeping on the couch where the man is sitting right now and cooking for her for a month before she takes the baby back to Shenzhen.

"What about the girl before you? Is she your sister?"

"Who? I don't know."

"A woman about your age who was also pregnant. When she had the baby, she disappeared. And the one before her? Your aunt must have lots of nieces."

To conquer the hard with the soft. But how? *What do you want?* Can she simply ask? Is it too hard a question? *Don't hurt me.* Is it too hard a request?

Or should she try the door? Head over to it, open it up, and cry out. But he will outpace her. He will sprint and shut the door before she reaches it. He will clasp her face, push her to the floor, knock her out, rape her, kill the baby. Is there murder in his eyes? She is not sure. She is still hoping he will turn this all into a joke. Just say, *Sorry, I'm pulling your legs. I'm just kidding. I'm* . . . all those English expressions for humor that Americans are so known for.

She is still being hopeful. That's all she can be. She had hoped Lao Li would divorce his wife, and when that did not happen, she hoped she would give him a son, and when it turned out to be a girl, she hoped she would get this done quickly, smoothly, go back, and try again to have a son. Or try something else. She will hope for something else. If there is nothing else, she will at least have a daughter. "At least you won't be lonely anymore," Lao Li said on the phone after she'd told him the baby's sex, which doctors in China would not let you know. That was all he had to say, and it is true: at least she won't be lonely anymore when her daughter is born. Now the question is how to get her daughter safely born.

The man watches her, waiting for her to make a move. That must be his strategy. She needs to pee. She feels a wet patch on her panty. She has been feeling it sporadically, just a drip, which can't mean that her water has broken. For the water to break, she thinks, there has to be more than a drip or two. If it is not pouring, it is squirting. Water where the baby swims. No anchor there, just a tiny, warm lake for her daughter to live. Who is listening right now, kicking, waiting for her to make a decision, a favorable one to alter the situation, to bring safety back to her, let her mature fourteen more days, until she's ready to come out. Then they will deal with the term *anchor baby*, a name already given to her.

"Do you want some water?" she asks. What's softer than water? She will get out of this spot, pinched between the couch and the TV stand, the man's big feet and long arms reachable to her belly. She will disturb the inevitability in the air. She can see a visible change in the man's eyes. He is taken by surprise. The mockery in his face is loosening its claws, its "hook-like arms."

"Yes, water would be good."

She turns toward the kitchen. He may follow her, corner her inside the kitchen, wave the kitchen knife and slice her open, or turn on the stove and burn her belly. There is no lock in the kitchen. And she needs to pee. She pauses by the kitchen door for just a second, walks on to the bathroom, and locks the door from inside. She sits down on the toilet and strokes her belly. She is alone with her baby here, at least. No intruder in this little room. She might need to give birth to the baby all by herself in this bathroom. She misses her mother. She wants to go back inside her, shut her eyes and dream, even though her mother would be just like her, not knowing what to do. Her mother has never quite known what to do, wearing the look of a lost child that she wants never to wear herself. How far she has come, from that dingy little town to Shenzhen, to America, but what difference does it make—to end up being cornered by a man, to be raped, her baby butchered. She will not let that happen to her. She has gone too far to let that happen. But here she is: the water sliding down her thighs, the warm, pinkish water her baby needs to swim in is abandoning her world. She bends over. It is happening: the water breaking, the cramps, the pain, while she is nowhere near a hospital, separated from her cell phone by a door and a man with contempt on his face.

But she needs to go to the hospital. She cannot imagine giving birth here all by herself. She will pay them cash. Where is her cash? The man could be ransacking her cash right now. Why did she let him in? She has no one but herself to blame if something goes wrong. Everything is already going wrong. Baby in distress. Is the baby still alive? It is still moving, agitated and unsure like herself. She wants to see her gynecologist, the Chinese American woman who carries herself with ease and confidence. She wants her daughter to be just like her one day, at home with her environment.

"Are you okay?" the man asks outside the bathroom door.

"I'm in labor," she cries. "I need to go to the hospital."

"I can help you," the man says after a pause, "I can take you to the hospital."

But she cannot trust him, cannot open the door and let chance decide her fate. She will have to do it all by herself. She is howling in pain now, making those awful sounds she does not believe she can make. "Go away. Leave me alone," she yells at the door in between moans. She will have to make it all by herself.

"I'll help you," he says again through the door.

But she will not trust him. She is all on her own now, depending on nothing but this one body that's splitting into two.

·

Does he mean it? Will he really help? He wants to help. He has helped her with her groceries, has told her she'd forgotten her key. He has no intention to hurt her. He just wanted a chat, about something that was bothering him, to get something off his chest. He is not a criminal. He has never hurt anyone intentionally. He has done nothing except ask a sensitive question so that she will tell him the truth. The truth—that is all he wants, a slight confession, when everyone keeps their secrets to themselves. He wants some truth. Maybe he will give her a piece of truth too, if she gives him one first. An exchange of truth between a man and a woman who would otherwise be total strangers. Nothing personal. Just the truth for once. But what is the point? No point maybe, just this final need to be mean, to be open. Is the only way for him to be open to be mean?

"Listen, I'm sorry I said those things to you. I want to help. Please trust me. I want to help you."

·

The pain is all there is. The rest ceases to matter. She is squatting on the floor now, which is wet, sleek with the same pinkish water that was inside her. The child is in there, with her big dreamy head: cry if she can, cry with her. She is moaning so loud she's deaf to it. She is unreachable. She is locked in her pain. No one can hurt her. She is protected by her pain. Her body feels nothing but the pain. That's all she is, the pain. She, the pain, and the baby who knocks her head on her life's edge, this thin edge.

·

What's he going to do? Leaning against the door that's locked from the inside, listening to a woman's horrible sound of giving birth, the sound you choose to forget the moment you come into the world. A mother's sound. His mother, dead for thirty years. You had a big head, your big head wouldn't come out, too big for me, they had to cut me open. I thought I was going to die. His mother who would say anything out loud, who pinned her suffering like a gold brooch on her chest, who talked and talked until he was gone, shipped to the war, no more on the receiving end of those verbal spits. You must not die. You must learn to stay alive. You can't be so selfish as to die on me. I've got no one else. Did she really say that? A mother to her only child whom she claimed to love so much she had to hurt. She just couldn't help it. It was not personal. It's not that I'm angry at you. It's only that I love you too much. If I didn't, I wouldn't have said all those things. It's your life, you know, no one else's. If you lose a limb, it's you who will live without a limb for the rest of your life. That's why I'm mad. I'm not going to be there to live with your lost limb for you. She is dead. He is here, with no lost limbs, but with something else missing, something harder to see. His mother knew but she pretended not to know. She would only see her own suffering reflected back to her, which made her angrier, at herself, at him, the extension of her suffering life. Let's die together. Let's drink this trembling glass of pain till it's over. Cheers.

Another birth. Another woman who has no idea what she is doing. Another child coming into the world pre-burdened with pain.

•

She must stay awake to this pain, not overcome by it, not slipping under. She must trust that her body knows what it is doing. Her body has outsmarted her again and again— conceived a child weeks before she even knew, made her throw up and then eat this and that so that the baby could grow, made her laugh and cry so that the baby could learn to feel, made her reckless and afraid so that the baby could have a will. The baby must be pushing too, with her little arms and legs and blind fists, beating, flailing, reaching for the light. She must follow her body, which is breaking itself.

•

Is the weeping from inside him? His mother had kept her last breath until she saw him. She had waited, with such a will, holding that tenuous, tenacious breath, to touch his hand, to tell him that she had loved him more than anything else in this world, despite everything, and he said, I know. He forgave her. Or maybe she didn't say anything, just looked at him, with those embittered eyes, so accustomed to bitterness that bitterness was in everything they saw. Eyes that looked at him, and then suddenly were looking at nothing. I've done my best, he read in her eyes. I wish I could have done better, but I've tried.

He slips to the floor against the door. His mother had pushed and pushed, and his head was caught in the narrow canal. He could have died, but was kept alive, brought to this moment to be a door apart from a birth taking place.

"You can do it," he says to the door. "Breathe, breathe."

He feels as if he is once again crawling in the birth canal, the strangling tunnel toward life, his mother's heart pumping blood, her moans drowning his own. He will make it out somehow, as there is no turning back.

·

She sees the crown, the creamy black moss. She takes loud, shuddering breaths as her body continues to push and break. She sees the earthy head, the close-eyed face, blood-streaked, stunned, wrinkly. The baby is skidding out, mouth agape, gasping for air.

From beneath her body, she takes hold of this red child, who tenses, gathering her might into a howl. An announcement or protest? For hunger or fear? She palms her lopsided head and puts her to her breast. The baby smells her, groping for her nipple, and latches on. She holds her there, rocking lightly. Their voyage has just begun.

MILK

The boy follows the man, eyes on his pants, and mumbles, "Sir, please buy a rose, buy a rose for your girlfriend." The man's legs move faster; the boy grabs one of them, wraps his skinny arms and legs around it and presses his small buttocks on the man's leather shoe and says the words again to the leg.

The spring afternoon has gone sultry, the air recalling the texture of rotten fruit. The man is on his way to a sales meeting. He did not meet his sales quota, and, before the child approached him, had been rehearsing his explanations in his head. He tries to shake his leg free, but the child tightens his grip. People circle past them: a few giggle; a few gape to see how he reacts. His face flushes. He bends down and snatches the child's wrists and tosses him away from his leg. The child looks up at his face for the first time, shocked, as though he has just realized that he was not merely dealing with a leg, but an unpredictable man several times his size. He must also have sensed what's coming: the man kicks him, the shoe landing on his small rib cage. The child flips over on the pavement, groans, curls into a ball, and cries, "Mama, Mama—"

A woman runs toward them on the pavement, yelling in some rural dialect the man can't quite understand. But judging by her tone, he is sure she's calling him names or cursing him in the worst possible way. She kneels down by the child, picks him up, and clasps him to her chest. The child's cry turns into wail; he looks as heartbroken as any other wailing child, though the pathetic rose is still clutched in his hand. The woman strokes his ribs. Sallow-faced, ill-dressed, she must have been lurking somewhere by the roadside, blending right in with other urban poor the man has stopped paying attention to.

People gather around them, gawking like their eyes have finally found a free feast. The man's head buzzes, his face grows hot. "Are you his mother?" he shouts down at the woman. "What kind of mother lets her child pester people on the street?"

Then he turns, quickly, not wanting to hear one single word from the woman. He walks away as fast and steady as his body can manage, controlling the impulse to run, and slows down only after he is sure the woman's gaze no longer reaches him. Then he breathes and it feels like the first real breath he has taken since he bent down to grab the child—his wrist thin like a chicken's neck. The man has never felt comfortable watching vendors wring chicken necks in the market. He will grimace and avert his eyes. I'm not a bad person, he imagines saying to the woman whose face still seems to hover right in front of him, its misery and rage so sharp that it reduces the dusty street, dusty plastic-looking palm trees, dusty pedestrians with their idiotic stares to nothing but a stage setting. I'm not a bad person. He imagines the woman's face softening and him taking a ten-yuan bill from his wallet and stuffing it in the child's grimy hand. Then, like an uncle, he will hold the child up and make faces at him till he laughs.

But he knows that's not what he will do. He will keep walking and rehearse his explanations for the failure to meet the sales quota and pray he keeps his job. That is all he can do and will do. He takes another breath. As the air infused with humidity, dust, and exhaust fills his lungs, the city distorts—its skyscrapers, shops, multi-lane streets, vehicles losing their edges and density, fattening with the incessant despairs and high hopes steaming out of people's heads. All around him the city is swelling, and his feet are hardly touching the ground. He has become a splinter the city is about to push out of its inflated flesh.

•

The woman carries the crying child to the side of the pavement, under a palm tree. The child murmurs, "Mimi, mimi." The woman sighs, lifting her blouse, and the child presses his mouth to her breast. People gawk and shake their heads. She lowers her eyes and sees their shoes— tennis shoes, leather shoes, canvas shoes, high-heels, sandals, flats—nice shoes that know where their feet are taking them. She shields the child's face with a hand: it's better he doesn't see any of these shoes, better still he forgets where they are. The blind fortune-teller told her that this was a hard time for them, but things would get better in three years. "Luck star will then shine above your son's head." The man raised his opaque eyes. She paid him five yuan and that was all she got—a promise of a turn of fortune in three years. Can she keep her milk flow that long? She felt foolish. She needed the five yuan for food, not a fortune that would not turn until three years from now. But still, three years is better than five or ten, or no luck at all.

She came to the city to look for her husband, whom she has not heard a word from since he left after the Spring

Festival. She called the construction company he worked for; they said they hadn't seen him since he'd left for home before the festival. She went to the village fortune-teller, giving him her husband's year, month, date, and hour of birth and, as payment, a bucket of frogs her son had helped her catch. The old man flipped the brittle pages of his yellow book, wrote down four columns of words with ink and brush, squinted his eyes at a brittle page again, and shook his head: "His longevity star is clouded this year. I see possible falling, a tall building, and serious or fatal injury." She held her breath. "A building in the south," he added, "in the city where he builds those tall buildings."

The woman took her son to the city. She found the construction company. They told her the same thing they had said on the phone. She told them what the fortune-teller had told her. They asked her to go talk to other construction companies. There are tons of them in the city, they told her, and her husband could be working for any of them now. She and her son wandered around the city, looking up at scaffoldings to see whether he was there. It was hard to tell. They all looked alike from down here—a helmet, a little torso, a pair of doll arms and legs. She waited with her son on the roadside for them to come down. She asked them about her husband. They shook their heads or mentioned another company or building under construction for her to check. At night, she and her son slept behind park bushes or under viaducts. She didn't want to go back to her village until she found her husband and warned him of his ill fortune ahead. She would make sure he went home with them, where there are no tall buildings and the inevitability of falling.

She had no money left so she begged. She tried to tell people her story, but they walked away. "They think we're fake," an old beggar woman from the same province told her. "They don't care about us, but some still pity children. Have your son sell flowers. That may still work." So she picked a less-bruised rose from a flower shop's trashcan and had her son sell it like other children on the street— except that people don't pity children either.

She has kept her milk flow for a time like this, a time that she always knew would come. The child's shoulders stop shuddering. His fingers loosen around the rose that lies by his feet like congealed blood. She looks up at the scaffolding across the street and the small figures of construction workers printed on the sky. Any of them can be her husband or could have been her husband. One dizzying misstep up there will be a step into the nothing down below, and if that happens, you won't even see his body.

She wishes she had a place to go, a private place where she could lie down with her son, close her eyes, enjoy this little pleasure of giving and taking, this little numbing sensation that is slowly spreading over her body. Any time now she's going to close her eyes. The shoes, legs, and wheels around them will disappear. She and her son will turn into some gossamer matter, hide somewhere in the air, until things get better for them.

•

A man is walking in this direction. He sees the mother and son on the side of the pavement under a palm tree. He takes out his smartphone from his messenger bag, pauses in front of them for a second, and snaps a shot. The woman doesn't even notice, her eyes drooped, her half-exposed breast coarse-skinned and sallow-colored like her complexion. The boy is obviously too big for this: he looks like he has tried his best to curl himself in her arms, but most of his legs still spill onto the pavement. Only the utter unselfconsciousness of his closed-eye suckling resembles that of a baby.

The man goes back to his apartment and makes instant noodles and sits down in front of his computer. He has recently started a blog called *Critical Eye*, a title he's having second thoughts about and considering changing into something less literal. He posts social commentaries, often in the form of snapshots he takes with his smartphone on the street. Though his blog has not gotten much traffic, he has noticed a quickening of his senses as he goes about his daily life. He is no longer a passive passerby, his life no longer a fuzzy parade of routines and a job that organizes his hours into rest, work, wants, and small gratifications.

Now he freezes moments he finds provocative, forms opinions, and makes them visible to anyone surfing his way. Sometimes, sitting in his cubicle or walking home from work, he feels he is simultaneously inhabiting the city and roaming a space ungoverned by gravity, where he's just about as free as one can be. But when he posts his blog entries, his photos and words gone public, he cannot help but feel an unease, a weak-hearted uncertainty that his posts will be scrutinized and attacked.

After he uploads the photo, he comments: "We are a decade into the 21st century and our country is becoming one of the strongest economic powers in the world, yet, here in our city that we claim to be a world-class metropolis, a woman is nursing a five- or six-year-old on the street as though they were in a remote 19th-century village. Why is this happening?"

He clicks Post and slurps his noodles. He was going to simply write, "This doesn't look good—nursing such a big child in public," but thought it would be too simplistic.

He checks some of the blogs and websites he frequents and then checks back to see whether he has gotten any comments. There are none. He surfs more and checks back again. Still none. No response is almost worse than a negative response. He thought this post would provoke: the photo alone should catch attention and his commentary should generate a public debate.

He puts his computer into sleep mode and goes to bed. He dreams of a woman lying so close to him he can feel the buzzing heat and electricity radiating from her body. It's his ex-girlfriend, who by now must have become someone else's wife and maybe even a mother. But somehow, she has come back to him. Has she kept a key to his apartment? Did she sneak in, tiptoe to his bed, and lie down by him? Gently, she palms his head with one hand and with the other cups her breast to his mouth. His penis swells up, and as her hand slides down him, he sucks on her nipple and milk flows out. The liquid only surprises his tongue for a second before it calls back an ancient euphoria—he feels as if he were soaring into a galaxy of burning stars and becoming part of its radiance and order, fervor and harmony. As he comes, he wakes up. His ex-girlfriend is not with him. He is alone in his small, stuffy room. His computer sits on the desk like a large toad. His dirty clothes litter the floor. The air smells of semen, sweat, and greasy hair. In his mouth he tastes nothing but fetid breath.

But still he remembers the smooth, luscious milk on his tongue and the wondrous feeling of soaring and peace. He closes his eyes and tries to will the true-to-life sensation back into being—his ex-girlfriend's flesh blended with his, her breast throbbing in front of his face. He opens his mouth, closes his lips around the nipple where the elixir will flow onto his parched tongue.

·

A woman surfing the internet stumbles upon the photo on the man's blog. She once lived in that city; now she is living abroad. Since she became a mother, she has wished she were there instead of here—if nothing else, she would at least have someone to talk to in her native tongue, another mother raising a child. The boy being nursed in the photo is much bigger than her son, who has finally fallen asleep on her lap. She is weaning him. She has nursed him for eighteen months, has suffered cracked nipples, plugged ducts, and bouts of mastitis. But her son's demand for her breasts has not dwindled. He wants to nurse before sleep, before nap, after sleep, after nap, during the middle of sleep and nap and during other activities. He grabs her breasts as if they were his. She wants her body back. She craves spicy food and caffeinated tea, wants to wear dresses, not nursing bras and breast pads. She wants her body to be touched by her husband, and when that happens, she doesn't want her breasts to leak milk.

Her husband is not at home again. Got some work to finish, he said on the phone. When he does come home, he sleeps on the couch in the living room, says he needs his sleep so he can get up and work and support the family. It suited her at the beginning, when she loved to snuggle with her son alone on the big bed, her body willingly letting its white ribbon of milk flow into his mouth, as though his intake was also her intake, her giving so complete it merged into taking. They were locked in the cycle of give and take, forming a circle with no beginning or end to allow another's entrance. When her husband touched her, she recoiled from the intrusion. When he held the baby, the baby screamed for her. He spends less and less time with them.

When she asks him to change the baby's diaper, or give him a bath, or take him out for a walk, "because he's your son too," he looks vexed. He fumbles the diaper on the baby loosely and poop leaks out and she has to wash him again. The walks he takes with the baby tend to be short, "because he was screaming the entire time and people thought I kidnapped him." Once she caught him holding the baby upside down, dangling in front of his legs, big-headed like a frog, with blood pooling in his puffy face, too startled or strained to make a sound. She had just finished her weekly shower and instinctively knew she needed to be gentle. She crouched down to take hold of the baby's head and eased him into her arms, putting his wronged face to her wet breast. "That's enough," she then said to her husband, still suppressing a scream in her throat. "Just leave!"

Maybe it's all her fault—she pushed him away. And it's all her fault, too, that the baby is addicted to her milk. Didn't she give him her breast when she wanted him to go back to sleep so she could sleep longer, give it when she wanted him to take a nap so she could rest, give it again when he was fussy so she could have some peace? She has been weaning him for weeks now, slowly cutting down the sessions, first daytime, then night. Now they've come to the last and most trying session—the one he has been depending on to fall asleep at night. Earlier, he battled with her, reaching for her breast, and when pushed away, reaching again. He bawled and whimpered. She stuffed cotton balls in her ears. She rocked and sang and yelled and patted him, until he finally drifted off in exhaustion.

She's surfing the internet because there is nothing else she can do right now. There is a lot to do—dishes need to be cleaned, toys need to be picked up, soiled clothes need to be washed, but she is afraid if she moves, the child will wake up and want to nurse again. The whole battle will repeat, and she's too tired for that. And she knows her breasts will be filling up soon. She will need to go to the bathroom sink and squirt the milk out instead of giving it to her son, who wants it so much and can't understand why his mother is denying him the very thing that she used to offer him so abundantly.

She sees the photo of the countrywoman nursing her big son on the street in the city where she used to live, and heat leaps up her eyes before she knows it. She looks at her baby: his lips open to a zero; his blue-veined eyelids tremble as though there is a storm below. She holds him to her face, crying as silently as she can. But the child wakes up, gazes at her, alarmed. He reaches his little fingers to her cheek, as if to find out through touch what she is actually doing. It must be an expression he hasn't seen much before, even though he has made it thousands of times in his one and a half years of life. He stares at her. He is about to cry himself, his little face already folding into those familiar creases. She tries to stop herself, wiping her eyes. "I'm okay," she says to him. "I'm okay." But she continues to shudder. Her milk is filling up. The child smells it and lifts his mouth to the breast close to it, but he hesitates, examines her face, afraid she will push him away again. Her cry must have something to do with that. He is making the connection. But it's all too much for him. His sorrowful face lifts to her breast. "Mimi, mimi," he pleads.

A DRAWER

1940s

Through the red veil, she sees her mother's red wrinkles, red tears sliding down her red cheeks, her groom's red wedding suit, red fingers touching red hem; she sees red river, red trees, red temple, red children grabbing her hands across a red doorsill.

They bow to the sky and the earth. The same sky that faced her when she lay in the wheat field in her childhood, the same earth that warmed her back, the two arches meeting on her left and right. She, a pea in a peapod: the pod expanded, the pea shrank.

They bow to her in-laws. They bow to each other.

Because of the war, her dowry has been traded for food

piece by piece. All gone except for the quilt her mother made for her.

"What if I don't like him?" she had asked then, holding the fabric and cotton in place for her mother to pull the needle.

"Learn to like, then you will."

"But how?"

"We're all humans, all have a heart that's made of the same material. How hard is it to like another?"

"But I don't know him."

"You will."

"What if my mother-in-law is mean?"

"Do what you're supposed to do and don't let her down. Don't let them down."

Her mother added another stitch. She imagined her heart stretched so large and thin that it held other hearts, all crimson and beating.

•

In the bedroom, he unveils her. The red peels away. In the shock of her cleared vision, she lowers her eyes and looks at the bedding her fingers touch and then at her small bound feet—bed and feet not quite her own. But here she is, where her body sits and ends, her body now being seen by someone else for the first time. She feels both small and expansive in her husband's eyes.

In her glances, his eyes too are shy. But because she still doesn't know him, he remains a stranger. His warm, moist hands move across her skin, a student's hands with ink stains and rough-cut nails that have held books and ink brushes. Her skin prickles. Her heart shivers and pounds.

•

He joins the army a month later, announces to the household that it is his duty to protect their country. All his education has taught him that way, he says. The large unit of nation must be privileged over the small unit of family. His father nods. His mother wrings her hands. She too wrings her hands.

Her eyes follow his uniformed body marching with other recruits out of the village gate.

She is left with the memories of his body, and the fear that it will bleed till his eyes no longer see and limbs no longer feel, or that it will shatter, intact only in her remembrance—his body that has held hers and has momentarily made her longing stop.

So many ways she sees him die, so many images of

death. She finds herself wanting to draw them so that they won't continue to duplicate like mildew in her head. She feels wicked to harbor these doomed images. She should instead focus all her visions on his return, on his intact self to be released from the war, which remains abstract except for the images she sees—the bloodshed, broken limbs, the ceasing-to-be.

•

Finishing laundry by the river, she picks up a stick to draw in the dirt. With each stroke, each wound she issues to the figures in her drawing, her heart jumps. Then she forgets about her heart. She draws and time goes by.

It is long past the hour to bring laundry home and cook lunch for the family. Her body stiffens when she hears a voice from above her head: "Good heavens! What are you doing?"

She turns. Her mother-in-law's face contorts, pupils widening as she peers at her drawing. There, miniature corpses lie about in the dirt: with gashes across chests, torsos without limbs, bayonets sticking out of bellies, fragmented heads.

"God!" The older woman now looks at her face, as though she can no longer recognize her. "What devil has got into you?" She stamps her feet, which are as small and bound as her own.

"I don't know," she mumbles while hastening to erase the drawing with her hands—the figures drawn in such horrific detail she too is shocked to see them.

As she stands up with the bucket of laundry, her mother-in-law's long-nailed fingers reach her face, pinch her cheek, and give it a hard twist. "You're heartless," she spits. "You're cursing men to die. You're cursing my son!"

She gasps in pain. "No, no, that's not true."

Letting her go, the old woman looks around them, at the cattails, the thistles, the ripples in the river and their reflections overlapping the ripples, as though to catch a glimpse of the evil spirit that might have been pinched out of her.

•

Her period does not come. She is seventeen and is going to be a mother. She does not know what it means and how she feels as a mother-to-be, except that her stomach is fuzzy and her body feels weighed down by nausea.

After dinner, she hears her ten-year-old brother-in-law recite the classic: "At the beginning of human life, its nature is kind." She wants to draw wavy lines, rippling lines. Her fingers want to move on a surface to create an image. But her mother-in-law has been watching her, warily, as though afraid she might be conspiring. She goes to her room and scribbles lines on her thighs with her fingertip. She opens the drawer that holds her husband's ink, brush, and rice paper, but knows better than to use them.

When her morning sickness lessens and her belly expands, she wants to draw circles and spirals. She wants to draw out this kindness supposedly buried in the beginning of life. What does it look like? A baby's unfocused eyes? Its little fingers moving like soft river plants? Its little mouth suckling? Where does this kindness lie? In its hard, oversized, lopsided head? Its faint but fast-beating heart the size of a walnut?

She draws in her head, imagining a scroll unroll into a piece of white paper on which she will use her husband's ink and brush to draw, to paint, from left to right, and even when she reaches the very end at the right, she will still be able to step back and see the whole picture. The whole piece. She will see the images travel and arrive from somewhere to somewhere. She will just sit there, stay perfectly still, except for her hand moving the brush. She will continue to draw until she can see the image of the beginning of life and its nature of kindness.

As her belly grows bigger, she draws there. Sometimes, a little finger will meet hers from inside.

And after her daughter is born, she draws on her back, which often quiets her, lulling her to sleep.

·

He comes back on a two-week leave for his father's funeral. No longer a boy, he is taller, thinner. He wears a beard and a medal on the chest pocket of his green army uniform. His skin looks coarse, features hardened into their places, his eyes weary. He spends most of his time with his mother. He lifts the baby up a few times, but each time she howls, and he hands her back. He sleeps with his back toward her after quick sex.

On the last day of his leave, as he rises from bed, she puts her hand on his arm: "Don't go back."

"I must." He stands up. "You don't know our enemy." His eyes darken. "They rape women and stab babies in the belly."

He leaves. And now it is her daughter's death that she sees day and night.

She carries her in a sling in front of her chest, so their hearts are beating together. Time and time again, she sees blood spray out of her round belly as the bayonet stabs in.

She knows she will die if that happens; she'll follow her baby's soul wherever it goes and guide it back to her. She knows she will, but she doesn't really know. She has never seen the world of souls. What if her small feet won't carry her fast enough?

She goes to the temple to pray. "Pity us," she says to the Guanyin statue. "Spare our lives. We have nothing but each other." The goddess does not respond. Dust gathers on her white stone gown.

She goes to the river and, with the baby suckling on her chest in the sling, picks up a stick to draw. She draws whirlpools, circles within circles, draws a round baby belly in the sand. She draws monstrous faces she has been evading in her head. She needs to draw to see them. She draws hands, bestial or skeletal, to know their strength. She will try to unfasten those hands to snatch her baby back, or kiss them for mercy.

•

When the child is three, the enemy surrenders, the war is over. He comes back but won't look at her or their daughter in the eyes. He sleeps fitfully still. He says he cannot stay long, needs to go back to his army: there is another war to fight—the civil war.

"Who are you fighting this time?" she asks.

"The enemy."

"Who are they?"

"Those who look like our countrymen but act just like the invaders we got rid of."

"Do they also rape women and stab babies?"

"They do, and until we defeat them, there will be no peace."

He does not touch her except for once, in the middle of the night when he is half asleep. On the last day of his visit, he takes out a piece of paper and a red inkpad from his green army bag and asks her to stamp her index fingerprint at the bottom of the paper. She asks what the words say—those little strokes neatly assembled together announcing something unknown to her. He says, Please, just do it. He looks at her pleadingly. He has never looked at her that way. She does it. He is gone again. Her period comes. Her mother-in-law watches her belly that remains flat.

She grows exhausted with fear. When she sees strangers coming to the village, she doesn't know whether they are the enemy or not. Her heart jumps at the slightest sound. Her head reels the moment her daughter leaves her sight. Her daughter has started to say no to her. She feels lonely when the child does it, feels betrayed somehow.

She is still nursing her, but the child wants her milk less and less, the milk that stitches them together. Her breasts grow drier and drier. She feels some part of her breasts has died and some part of her brain has died too.

She tries to draw simple things: a bird, a fish, a dragonfly. She shows her daughter how to draw them in the dirt by the river. But her heart does not feel the peace that the simple drawings should bring.

·

Three years later, a letter comes from her husband. He has become an officer and has married a comrade who has borne him a daughter and is pregnant with a second child. They have settled down in the city. He has found a job for his younger brother there and hopes his mother will join them too. As to his *ex*-wife, she is free to stay in their house or move back to her own family. She has been free since she stamped her fingerprint on the divorce paper. He is sorry, he says in the letter, but their marriage was arranged. They had no common language.

Her brother-in-law, who is now a young man, reads the letter with his head bent, never once looking up. Her mother-in-law looks at her at the mention of fingerprint and divorce paper, her eyes frenzied and frail. She turns toward her room, stumbling as though she has forgotten how to walk.

Soon, a woman with big feet and clipped hair comes to the village, her army uniform cinched at the waist with a buckled belt. In the center of the village square, she announces that women are free now. No more bound feet, no more arranged marriage, no more slavery at in-laws' house, no more discrimination against baby girls. Women, she announces, are equal as men, can hold up half of the sky.

She goes home on her small feet that she knows cannot be stretched back to their natural size.

•

Her brother-in-law leaves for the city. Her mother-in-law will not leave her bed. The food she serves stays untouched. Then come the drooling mouth, the hanging jaw, the wooden eyes. She feeds her with a spoon. She checks for her breath every morning.

She takes the brush, ink, and rice paper out of the drawer. Now, she is using them, as she had dreamt of doing when she wanted to draw out the kindness of human nature. She draws her husband standing by a woman with big feet and clipped hair, in a city background that she has never seen—asphalt streets, brick buildings, buses and bicycles—but can somehow imagine. She brings her drawing to her mother-in-law, who cannot or will not move her face, so she moves it for her. But she only detects a minute disturbance, or maybe nothing at all. She feels lonely now that she is alone to bear the desertion. She balls up the drawing and stuffs it in the stove, burns it while preparing dinner, so that when her daughter comes back from school, she will not see it. She sees the rice paper curl into a dark phantom. The images that occupied her head, the curses she wanted to direct their way, him and his comrade, the literate city wife, burn to ashes in the stove she cooks dinner on.

She feeds her mother-in-law congee, wipes her mouth, cleans her body, changes her bed. Sometimes, she holds her hand and talks to her, as she was unable to do when her own mother passed away several years ago. She looks at her face, which is now almost translucent, the lines resembling those on the river surface when breezes brush by.

One day, when she finishes a drawing of her mother-in-law's face, she drinks some water, comes to her side to feed her, and feels her cold lips.

Her death looks so similar to her last year of life she finds it hard to believe that her stasis has concealed a movement, the final one, the final step into the other realm. She must have been inching toward it like an old turtle, patiently approaching without leaving any trace, without even changing her facial expression. How resolute she must have been, and how persistent in her resolution.

She steps back to look at her drawing lying flat on the table and realizes that what attracts her about her mother-in-law's face is not its transience, but its acceptance, its readiness to submerge into the water of the dead, quietly, effortlessly, without the slightest splash.

"At the beginning of human life, its nature is kind," she listens to her daughter recite the classic. Eventually, we shall all go back to that beginning state of kindness, she thinks.

•

Again, she starts to draw simple things: fish in the river, chicken in the yard, plants in the garden, willow by the window, finch on the willow . . . She looks at them as she washes clothes, feeds the chicken, and tends the vegetable garden. She looks at them and thinks of the brush strokes she needs to put on the paper so their images will emerge the way they are—simple, singular, alive, suspended in a moment in time.

And when she is able to do it just right, with the right

amount of ink, tone, and shade, with the right strokes of energy and precision, the images will float out of the paper as if on an exhaling breath, and then she will feel a peace she seldom feels.

On the thin rice paper, she draws, with fewer and fewer strokes, a bird flying from white to white, river grass ascending the air, a fish swimming across seasons. They are still and they are in motion. When winter arrives, she draws a little plum flower at the end of a sword-shaped branch. She comes to stand by it and, for a moment, her heart feels like a scroll of moon-white space that opens, and is edgeless.

WENCHUAN

When the earth shakes, we balance ourselves in paddy fields, on pig farms, on mountain paths, at roadside stalls, in salons washing customers' hair, massaging their feet, applying nail polish, at home making cattail baskets, preserving bamboo shoots, embroidering shoe insoles. Then we think of our children. We run toward their schools—past uprooted trees, crooked, crumbling buildings, past screaming, weeping people, past debris and gashes on the streets. We see other parents running in the same direction.

.

We dig. For days we dig until the soldiers come. Then we carry our children's portraits and wait. Each time we close our eyes, we are still digging.

Some of us find our children's bodies and bury them in the woods behind the schools. We salvage a door from somewhere to mark their graves, or a bedspread, a few bricks, a few wood boards, a plastic bouquet of flowers. We carve our children's names on the wood, on the brick. We kneel down and burn incense. Some of us do not get to bury our children's bodies. They are taken to the crematoria, several of them shoved into the oven together, and we have to split the ashes among us. We bury them in one place and take turns to come and mourn. Maybe it's fine: they will not be too lonely here; they have friends to play with.

•

Some of us never get to see our children's bodies again. They remain buried under the rubble, cordoned off with yellow tape and patrolled by security guards. Some of us still hear our children calling faintly from underneath— the four stories' worth of debris, four stories of bricks, slabs, and beams piling on top of them. Some of us see a small waving hand, a shape that looks like a face, a black spot gazing like an eye. We tell the guards not to stop us and walk onto the rubble that collapses, breaking and powdering under our feet. We call our children's names. We mark a clear spot by the rubble, put a stone there, and carve our children's names on the stone. The sky is the color of iron, hanging low, like it's halfway fallen.

·

Many of us live in the tents. Some of us eat the instant noodles or the hardtack the relief workers distribute to us. Some of us see children, rice paper thin, rising from the rubble, the graves, and floating footless above the ground, looking. What are they looking for? We save our relief food and put bottled water and apples by their stones, but there are so many thirsty, hungry children and not enough water and food. We cannot sleep. We get up in the middle of the night, needing to bring them more.

·

Some of us cannot forgive ourselves. One keeps saying had she let her daughter quit school and go to Chengdu with her, she'd still be alive. One says that the day before the earthquake, she had scolded her son for skipping classes to play computer games and he had listened to her and decided

to be a good student. The children must have sensed something, but we did not listen to them. There were so many
signs: rats showing themselves in the kitchen, dogs bark-
ing and cats screeching without a reason, and the burn in
our stomachs, the churn in our chests. The children had
insisted: *Ma, I don't want to go to school. I'm tired. I'm not
feeling well.* But we thought that was just another excuse.
We did not trust our own children.

•

Some of our husbands blame us. Some drink. One sits
leaning against a tree, which stands strangely green and
unbroken. Many lie with us in our cold tents at night and
think of what life is like for our children now. But no matter how hard we try, we cannot quite imagine the place
they have gone, or imagine them as anything but scared
and lonely in that place. We close our eyes and try to feel
that pain, falling from the third or fourth or fifth story,
being buried instantly by all those floors or ceilings. We
try to feel that pain so we could be there with our children
during that hour, that day.

•

The troops covered in white plastic suits and goggles come with bulldozers. They walk like astronauts. They tape off the entrances to the woods up the mountains where some of our children's graves lie. They say they come to disinfect and ask us to wait outside. When they are gone, our grave markers are gone too—the doors, the bricks, the bed-spreads we put on the graves, the names, the flowers, the bottles of spring water, all gone. That had to be done, the cadres come to tell us. Our Party puts people first. These bodies were buried too shallow. They would cause a plague if the fluid of the corpses flowed into the river. The cadres say they did it for our own good, say they labeled each body with a number, that they were careful with where each body was buried and didn't pile the bodies up; in-stead, they put them side by side a meter apart. They say we should not spread rumors.

·

Some of our husbands are construction workers. They find no reinforcement bars in the debris. They find the slab floors are hollow. They sneak into the taped-off rubble at night and take with them rebars thin as chopsticks and bricks crumbling like crackers. We go to the town hall, the education bureau, the county government. It's an earthquake, one official tells us, a magnitude-eight one. Buildings collapse in strong earthquakes like this. It's a natural disaster, beyond human control. We yell at him: Why didn't the buildings around the schools collapse—that shopping center right next to Longyun Middle School, that apartment complex by Yihong Elementary? Why did the schools alone collapse instantly? Another official searches for words, but what comes out of his mouth makes us gasp: What's the use? Even if everyone responsible were caught and shot, it wouldn't bring back your children. We make fists. We jump over him. We could have beaten him to death had the security guards not started beating us. Another official tries to explain: the government had waged a campaign—anti-illiteracy among the rural poor. Orders were issued: schools must be built in every township, ten here, twelve there. They borrowed from banks, asked for donations, hired the cheapest construction companies that in turn hired the cheapest laborers. It was like squeezing oil from a mosquito. He kneels down in front of us. He says he is sorry, says he should not have done what he did. He says he will bow his head to the ground for our lost children. He is crying. Our anger suddenly loses its strength.

·

They build long tents on top of the rubble and call them the "tent schools." They ask surviving students to the opening ceremony. Cameramen come, reporters. They wear masks, pull them down to give commands and then pull them back on again. This program will be shown on the Central TV No. 1 Program on June 1, the International Children's Day, at 8:00 p.m., they say. You will all be there, your faces on TV, shown to the whole country. They try to hold us back, but some of us get in the tents. We hold our children's portraits, their schoolbooks and award certificates. The director is leading the students to sing the national anthem: *Arise, you who refuse to be slaves* . . . This isn't a school, we say to these people holding cameras and note-books, these city folks wearing masks who do not want to breathe in the death of our children. This is a graveyard!

.

We come again to the county government, staggering through the miles of mangled land. Even children scavenging in the debris look bruised, their eyes gray. Even the fruiting apple trees look like they are cracking inside. The wrought iron gates are latched shut. We rattle the bars, shout at the square government building. It's been driz-zling for days. Our faces are wet. The drab sky, the muddy sun. A police car and a truck of soldiers in fatigues and helmets come. Listen to me, says the officer who steps out of the car and sweeps his eyes across us. You must trust the government: let the government solve the problems for you. What you are doing here disrupts social order, causes social unrest. It is illegal. If you don't leave, you must come with us. He points his finger at the truck and the soldiers clutching batons. Some of us fall silent, letting our arms hang. Some of us mumble something under our breath. Some shuffle our feet. Some stand still. The officer steps over to us. Sisters, he says, go home now. What's the use of standing here in front of the government and making a scene? Do you just want to make things even messier than they are? You think it's not enough that tens of thousands of people have just died, and you have to make things even worse? Now, go home and mourn for your children there. Some of us leave. Some of us are hauled onto the truck, sprawled on the tumbling floor, the sky askew with its ashen clouds. They dump us at the police station and the commissar, a woman with red eyes, says to us: I understand your feelings. I truly do. I lost a niece in one of the schools. But the government has done so much and has so much to do still. So many people have lost their lives, their families and homes. We can't only think of ourselves. We must think of the province as a whole, the country as a whole, and trust the government will do the right thing. Then she hands each of us a paper to sign, to promise we won't demonstrate again.

.

They send counseling teams. An older woman speaking Beijing dialect asks us to "reenact" the excavation scene, to talk about it: how we were feeling, how we are feeling. She asks us to sing, to do a strange city dance. Many of us refuse to go back. We would rather go visit our children's graves in the woods, even though we do not know if the soldiers have indeed put the right bodies in them. Or the communal burial sites where the ashes of our children are mingled together. Or the cemeteries built upon the old school ruins. We'd rather sit by these graves, talking to our children. Or lie in our tents, not moving. When we move, we wander into places where we will be alone. One of us jumps off the Unity Bridge into the Min River on a misty dawn. One of us swallows a bottle of insecticide and lies down under a dove tree that is yet to bloom. One of us disappears in the mountains for three days, until her husband and a search party find her sitting on a cliff covered in clouds.

.

They say we can have another baby. Some of us have had our tubes tied. Some of us are in our forties. Many of us cannot get pregnant. They let us try test-tube conception, twice for free, in the provincial capital. We take the five-hour bus ride to the hospital. Many of us continue to bleed. We continue to visit our children's graves. We burn incense, burn paper money, paper houses: *Buy whatever you want over there.* Our aging, grieving bodies are not able to make babies. We are not cows or hens. But still many of us try. We press into our husbands' bodies. We weep as we push and pull. We lay there in our exhausted breath. We try to imagine having a future again. Some of us carry a baby to full term; many of us miscarry. Some of us lose pregnancies to a cold, because we only have one relief blanket through the winter. Some of us lose them to malnutrition, because all we have to eat are hardtack and instant noodles. We carry the baby for a few weeks, a few months, then it is gone.

•

They say this is all part of the reconstruction. They say we are moving forward. We are building model cities on the old rural ruins. Now we are living the city life, moving into these brand-new apartment buildings. But we continue to get lost. We cannot remember where our unit is. We panic among all this concrete, which had broken our children's spines. We get dizzy in the staircases, put our keys in the wrong locks. We miss our old plots of land, the smell of dirt, of rapeseed flowers and cucumbers thickening on the vines. The reporters pour in before the anniversaries. They make us hold our new babies and take photos, which they then show in the newspapers and on TV, to the province, the country, the world. They make us talk about what we have been through and what we look forward to. Many of us keep our doors shut, or if they keep knocking, we say we have nothing to say. Some of us are afraid to say no. Some of us cannot say no, because our husbands were given a job in the Reconstruction Office. The reporters move their cameras around in our apartments: Let's try this angle, which makes the living room look bigger. You three sit there on the couch, your new son in the middle. Or, you two, just the two of you, but let's cook three dishes and one soup for dinner. Not bad, right? Three years after the loss. You have an apartment. You have each other. Your husband drinks and drinks. You embroider numerous shoe insoles. You keep the TV on.

•

We have nightmares. We are inside the schools. Chunks of concrete hail down around us. Our children call *Mama* and we call back. Stumbling through debris and dodging falling slabs, we follow their thin voices. We pull away the piling rubble with our hands. The bits and pieces crumble into powder as we touch them. We dig until our arms are too heavy to lift. We want to call out for help, but there is no one except for the other parents, scattered among the piles of debris, kneeling like us, digging with their hands toward their children. Our children's voices grow fainter. We bend our heads to the rubble, putting an ear to the crack where their voices drift. Sometimes our dreams have different endings. Sometimes we hear a low growl forming somewhere deep below, turning louder as it travels up: the rubble beneath us starts to tremble, the way the earth trembled beneath our feet that afternoon. The growl surges into a roar, as though a large, furious creature is about to shake the earth open, once again—but this time, to blast away the piles of debris and clear a tunnel for our children and us to see each other. Now comes a final blast and we are tossed into the air. And there in the air, we see a green field pulsing with wildflowers where our daughters and sons are running toward us, and our bodies come back to life.

·

Many of us leave, if we can. To Chengdu, Wenzhou, Shanghai, Shenzhen, to work in the factories, the shops, the salons. We continue to think of our children, as we move the fabrics up and down the needles of the sewing machines, as we put stuffing in the stuffed animals, as we assemble electronic parts, as we bend over customers' feet or massage soap into their hair. We repeat. We work until our fingers are numb and we keep working.

·

Some of us have burned our petitions: *It's useless—they are not going to do anything.* Some of us continue to send our petitions to the county government, the provincial capital, to Beijing. They send cadres back to talk to us, who call us sisters and follow us around, asking us to sign a paper, to be patient, to wait, to not make trouble. They tap our phones. They try to stop us from boarding a bus or a train headed to the capital, to stop us from appearing in front of the government buildings. But we continue to appear, carrying our children's portraits in front of our chests.

We point out the portraits on the gravestones to our new daughters or sons, who are now almost the same age as our lost children: That is your older brother. That is your older sister. Where is she? our new children ask. Year after year, it's time to visit this silent sister, this motionless brother lying under the stone. Our silky-haired daughters, our shiny-eyed sons. We will not think of them as dead. They are living with us. A red sun is again falling behind the mountains, which have turned green again except for the bald patches where trees had been cut down. But trees will come back; it is people who stay gone. Their bones remain for the mountains to grow.

●

Many of us start a vegetable garden in the mountains. We clear the brambles, turn the soil, sow the seeds, water them, see them sprout two leaves, then four, like a baby's cell. We eat the fresh vegetables from our own gardens and sell the extra on the streets to help pay our rents. We feel the most peaceful when we are alone in the mountains. The dove trees are flowering again, with their large winglike petals flapping in the wind, and among so many white wings, our children come back to us. We talk to them. We teach them how to tend the gardens. We weed together, trim the surrounding branches and bushes for more sunlight, build trellises with sticks and twines for the green beans and tomatoes to climb, build fences to stop the rabbits and deer. We clear more brambles, turn more soil, sow more seeds. And at the end of the day when we have to leave, our children say to us: *Ma, I don't want to go to school tomorrow. I want to come here with you and tend this garden.* And we, our hands covered by dirt, noses by the smell of green things, tell them: *You don't need to go. You can always come here with me. You never need to go again.*

WINGS

On a spring day at dusk, walking out of the neighborhood woods with her husband, Lulu sees a winged creature on an apartment balcony in front of them. It looks like a bird but has no feathers: what is left of its wings resembles two half-opened folding fans without their silk mount. Its back is toward them, head bent low. It turns slowly, ponderously, as though it's trying to warm its brittle bones in the sun. But the sun is setting, and the balcony is shrinking around it.

Lulu glances sideways at her husband, who is talking about an article he has just read, something about ice melting, ocean surface rising, cities that will be flooded. She looks back at the creature: it is still turning, its face unrevealed, which she imagines to be as frail as its movement and decayed as its wings. After they reach the corner of the building, it still has not turned all the way around.

As they approach the exit of the apartment complex and head toward their own, the creature appears again, walking slowly in front of them, dragging its worn-out wings that now, closer, look metallic and rusty, as if they have been through great fires in addition to great ages. At the exit, it turns around, and Lulu sees a human face in front of those wings, a little girl's face.

Do you want to know me? the child asks in a language Lulu understands, her serious eyes fastening to Lulu's.

Lulu glances again at her husband, who is still talking about the imminent flood. As she returns her gaze to the child, she notices that one of her hands is not quite a hand, but more like a bird's foot, with claws, not fingers. The rest of her body appears just like a child's and is naked and half shielded by her ruined wings. Lulu does not know what to say. With her husband, she walks on.

A dozen steps away, she looks back. The little girl is squatting on her heels on the side of the pavement, her bleak wings draping onto the ground. She holds a twig and draws something in the dirt.

•

Back at their apartment, Lulu sits down on the couch and turns on the TV. She flips through the channels until she sees the image of a dead child lying in the fetal position in a ditch, feet and hands tied with black shoelaces. A documentary—the boy had been reported missing and "the autopsy showed ample evidence of trauma and sexual assault," says the reporter in his trained grim voice.

Lulu finds such shows abhorrent but cannot take her eyes away from them. Nor can she take her eyes away from those posters of missing children on the walls—at bus stations, subways, grocery stores, post offices—the little faces, columns of data, brief descriptions: a four-year-old in polka-dot tights and green Tinker Bell sandals, a seven-year-old in a yellow t-shirt and white Nike sneakers, one with a birthmark below her left ear, one with a mole above his right brow. Looking at them, Lulu feels as if the world is turning into quicksand, sucking those children in until all that's left of them are these flat photos of lost smiles.

She turns off the TV. Her husband is still looking at his computer by the dinner table, earphones on.

Lulu goes to the bathroom. In the mirror, her face looks tentative, her eyes faintly pleading. She smacks her face between her hands, harder than one does to get some color in their cheeks. But the burn is slight, innocuous, then gone.

She turns the shower scalding hot and gets in. As the water burns down her skin, she thinks of the winged child she alone saw: little, cannot be more than five, but with such a pensive face. What are those fossil wings? How did they grow onto her thin shoulder blades? And the bird foot?

She finishes her shower, says good night to her husband, and goes to bed. In the dark, the winged child's question rings in her ear: *Do you want to know me?* Nobody has asked her a question like that before, except maybe when her husband asked her to marry him ten years ago—but it didn't seem to carry the same urgency, as though her refusal would sadden him beyond repair. Or maybe it did, and she has just forgotten. All these years of marriage have worn that moment out. Sometimes she wishes one of them would have the courage to say to the other: *Let's have a child. Let's not worry about anything.* When they make love—which they are doing less and less—she hopes he would say it, or she would, and he would say *Yes.*

She feigns sleep when her husband lies down by her. Soon his breathing evens out. She fights the urge to get up and take sleeping pills, which she's becoming dependent on, the way her mother used to be. She takes a deep breath and the bird-child resurfaces—crouching there on the roadside, the child draws with a twig, her wings softer then, draping like winter willow branches.

•

The next day, having lunch with a colleague in their firm's high-rise café, Lulu sees something emerge from a pool of fluorescent lights and computer screens in the glass building across the street. It's the same bird-child, who steps to the building's transparent wall, her wings closed around her. She looks down, pressing both her hand and claws to her chest, as if afraid of heights—will her spent wings spread and bear her up, or will they only make her plummet faster?

"Do you see that?" Lulu asks her colleague, who is about her age and has two children.

"See what?"

Lulu points at the winged child who looks like the only being alive in that building.

"I don't see anything," her colleague says.

The child steps back into the maze of electric lights and cubicles. Then she disappears. The building now looks devoid of life: its hundreds of feet of laminated glass blankly reflect the other buildings, the gray sky, gray clouds, the light rain aimlessly falling.

Back in her cubicle, Lulu cannot think of anything but the child. Is she an illusion or an apparition, haunting her alone?

Her boss left his laptop in a cab during his lunch break. "All my important documents are in there," he says.

Lulu calls the taxicab company's lost and found. She files documents, makes photocopies, takes phone calls. All the while, she looks around for the winged child. She goes to the bathroom, half expecting to see her when she opens a stall door. Or see her reflection in the mirror when she looks up from the sink. She imagines a message typing itself on her computer screen, like in the sci-fi movies. *Do you want to know me?* Letters pop up one by one. But all the messages she gets are either from her boss or for him.

Taking phone calls, she hopes to hear the child's voice, in a language not quite hers but that she somehow understands. It must be like a baby's understanding of her mother tongue. But the phone calls too are either from her boss or for him. She answers them, nods her head, mutters, "Yes, yes."

•

On the subway home, she looks at the door each time new passengers step on, and after the door closes, she looks at their reflections in the windowpane, hoping to see the little face and the despondent wings emerge, wings that seem to do nothing but weigh the child down.

Years ago, when Lulu was a child, her babysitter went out to run some errands one day, leaving Lulu alone with her teenage son. He asked her whether she wanted to make a phone call to her mother. She said yes and he took her to his room. "Let's pretend this is a telephone booth," he said unzipping his jeans and pulling her hand to his crotch. "Let's pretend this is your phone."

After her mother picked her up, later than usual, and apologized to the babysitter, Lulu didn't tell her what had happened. She didn't want to look at her mother either. In that shuttered, airless room where her babysitter's son hovered over her, she'd called out to her mother in her head to come save her, but she didn't hear.

Sometimes on the train, like today, after the busy stops are passed and most passengers have gotten off, Lulu wishes the train would run on forever. Then she wouldn't need to do anything; she would just sit there, her body slowly acquainted to hunger, to immobility.

Her mother, who had come from China thirty years ago, in the hold of a cargo ship, carrying her in her belly, must have felt that way when she finally took the bottle of sleeping pills. Hopped onto the train of sleep. The train started and would not stop. When Lulu closes her eyes and holds her breath, she can almost see her mother—lying there in the train made of air that is still orbiting the earth.

·

The next morning, she feels ill. She calls the secretary line, leaves a message, and turns off her cell phone. She lies in bed, feeling as though she is being shoved into a crack of the world and she must not move, or her lungs would burst, her bones shatter. She must quietly shrink to a smaller size. Then maybe her body would simply disappear.

Her dreams are nightmares, colonized by small torn bodies, trembling limbs, muffled cries. She wakes to a spasm in her chest, afraid to close her eyes again. She looks around and says to the room, *Yes, I want to know you*, first silently, then out loud. She holds her breath to listen, waiting for the invisible to turn visible. *But how?*

She gets up, stumbles to the bathroom. Removing a razor from her shaving kit, she curls her left hand into a fist, slaps her wrist like a nurse does, and then puts the razor's edge on the bulging veins. But she is not going to do it. She will not leave her husband the mess—police report, funeral arrangement, heartbreak. She will save this for later, like her mother who saved it until she had grown up, with no obligations left.

Still holding the razor, Lulu takes some gauze pads from the cabinet and sits down on the toilet seat. She surveys the skin on her arms and legs, closes her eyes for a moment to remember, and then starts carving on the flat surface of her right thigh. A glinting sensation issues from the incision, jolting her body out of its languor. The dull ache in her head and muscles fractures, crumbles, dissipates into sweat beads that bloom on her forehead. She presses a gauze pad down to stanch the blood, closes her eyes to focus on the pain—so fresh she can't imagine ever slicing her wrist with the razor, turning her body into an unfeeling mass.

She goes on, pausing only to wipe her eyes, which are running with the surges of pain. The size of a palm, the engravings on her flesh are two sets of slanted bars that converge at the top. They do not look like wings. No one will associate them with flight. But they are burning with such fervor they seem to be gathering a tremendous will to take to the air.

•

She covers the cuts with a clean gauze pad, drinks some water in the kitchen, and returns to bed. The child's dead wings, heavy, dense, refusing to dissolve, are now on her thigh. With her palm on the wound, she closes her eyes again. This time, she sees bird-child creatures scatter around the city—on the streets, in the markets, parks, restaurants, office buildings. Dispersed among the human population, dragging their flightless wings, they plod on. Lulu recognizes some of the faces: they are the same as those missing children on the posters, children of different hair, eye, skin colors, one with a birthmark below her left ear, one with a mole above his right brow. None of them are smiling.

Lulu opens her eyes momentarily to the afternoon sun pooling on her bed. When she closes her eyes again, she sees the same creatures in a forest. They walk silently through shaded branches, tangled vines, thorny undergrowth, and rays of sunlight cutting through the canopy. In the distance lies a lake. The winged children are traveling toward it. They can't see it yet, but know it is there.

Her husband comes home from work. She pulls down her pajamas to cover the cuts. He asks how she is feeling. "Better," she says.

•

The next morning, locking herself in the bathroom, Lulu opens the gauze pad to find that the cuts have scabbed.

They hardly hurt anymore unless she presses on them. Soon, maybe a day or two, the scabs will turn rusty and fall off and new skin will surface and blend in with the rest. And then there will not be a sign of those engraved wings. Even now, less than a day later, she can hardly remember the refreshing pain she felt when she made the cuts.

She peels the scabs. The cuts open again one by one.

She goes to work. On the train, in her cubicle, she puts her palm on her thigh, feeling through her skirt the gauze pad and the cuts underneath. She imagines the wings lifting up from her skin, expanding as she shrinks, clutching her own shoulder blades. She is among the winged children, wandering the city.

During her lunch break, she goes to the park near her office and eats her carryout. A pigeon paces over, orange-eyed, cooing hunger. The sun shines on its iridescent feathers, on new leaves of willows and tulips that open like spatters of blood. She puts her palm on her thigh and closes her eyes behind her sunglasses.

What does the sun feel like? a voice says. It's right by her ear, but when she turns her head, she sees nothing.

It feels warm, she says.

I can't feel it, the voice says, *but I like how you feel it.*

Lulu reaches for the child, or the source of the child's voice, but touches nothing.

Her boss asks to see her in the afternoon. The sun pours in through his two large windows.

"Have you found my laptop?" he asks, his voice a dark wedge in the sunlit room. "You need to try harder!"

Lulu feels a rustle of air, a small hand brushing her hip. She is suddenly dizzy with anger. "It's not my fault that you lost your laptop!" She puts a hand behind her back for the child to hold. "And I don't like the way you treat me. It's rude."

The shock on her boss's face makes him look small and wrinkly in the poured-in sun. Then he blinks and stares at her. She returns his stare without a flinch, struck by the same glinting sensation as when the razor sliced open her skin.

"It's not personal," he says finally, looking away.

As she walks out of his office, she feels a small hand curl in hers. After she sits down in her cubicle, a slight weight settles on her lap.

•

That night, she lies in bed and waits for her husband to finish his shower. The child is not with her. She is walking in the forest, in her head a blue lake. When her husband comes to bed, Lulu reaches for him, his skin moist.

His hand moves to her gauze pad. "What happened?" he asks.

She puts her hand on top of his. "I want to have a child," she says. "Let's have a child."

The lake ripples, moon-filled. The child walks toward it, quietly as if treading air.

It's all like a dream that Lulu might have dreamed as a baby, when the world was still tender like a newly hatched chick, metamorphic and without malice. A dream she might have dreamed but cannot remember or believe it was ever possible. Lulu sees the lake, so clean. The child steps onto its shore and looks down at the water.

CRAZY ENGLISH

Yun is at the letter *p, practicable, pragmatism, precarious*... She has precariously passed her TOEFL and is now preparing for the GRE. She has a plan. She will get into a graduate program in Chinese and then get a job teaching Chinese, and once she is all settled, she and Allen will perhaps adopt a child. The man, whom Allen calls a stalker, is not in her plan. This man tracks her down at the library and the bookstore and stares at her like a beast of prey. He can get hold of her, she knows, which is why she stays at home and keeps the shades shut. She waits for Allen to come home, and when Allen makes love to her, she wonders what the man would do if he cornered her, what if that man instead of Allen were on top of her. She has been at the letter *p* for days now, ever since that man, the stalker, entered her vision. She cannot look around without seeing him and the things he could do to her.

•

His eyes are bulbous, fast moving but steady—even when they dart around, they seem to be fixed on her. His face clean-shaven, puffy, glossy. His hair a crew cut, a patchwork of gray and beige, combed forward and sprayed stiff. He could be anywhere from thirty to fifty.

She is at the public library when she first sees him—at the very beginning of the letter *p*, appreciating with a certain despair the neatness of the words lining up in front of her, each slight shift signifying an entirely different meaning. She is in her late thirties and her brain grows a crust when it comes to learning language. At this age, she also doesn't expect anyone to stare at her like this man behind the reference shelf across the aisle—his eyes darting away as though stung, only to dart back the moment she lowers her eyes. It is a bewildering kind of stare that makes her blush and shudder at the same time.

When she looks up again, the man drops his entire upper body behind the shelf. From the corner of her eyes, she sees his black trousers pop out in the aisle. He moves toward her, his eyes held high, chest pushed out. He walks past her. Chills crawl up her back. He walks past her again, barely brushing her elbow. Two steps away, he swivels on one foot: "May I sit here?" He points at the empty chair by her, his voice quivery, light bouncing off his bulging eyes.

She glances around: all the desks are taken—some people appear to know each other, some do not. She gives a faint nod. He sits down and opens a thick book he must have removed from the reference shelf. She continues to copy GRE words, *pacifism, palatable, palpitate* . . . You can teach Chinese here, Allen told her when they were dating online. People are getting really interested in learning the language. And that is what she has been working toward: after all the hurdles, she will stand in front of a class of American students and say, Unlike English, Chinese words at least try to resemble or indicate what they mean.

She jerks when the man suddenly turns toward her. He stands up, circles behind her, throws a gum wrapper in the trash bin on her other side, and while doing so, he hovers above her like a standing bear. She freezes as if to play dead, holding her breath, telling herself it's time to go, but she's afraid to move, as if any movement will expose her further.

After the man repeats the same motion, hovering even longer above her this time, she bolts up out of sheer will, scuttles out of the library into the glare of the late-afternoon sun that peeks out over a cluster of office buildings. Her eyes throb. At the first traffic light, she looks back: he is not behind her, but she can't be sure—he could have dodged behind a tree, a bush, a car, or into a doorway the moment she turned her head.

She scurries past houses with lawns and flowers. This has been her favorite stretch of walk, but it looks specious now, like it is a façade, a stage prop in a silent movie, and she sees herself: a panicked foreign woman rushing past the pretend tranquility.

She and Allen live in a Chicago apartment complex reminiscent of the utilitarian constructions during the Mao era. Theirs is a one-bedroom, a room less than the condo she once owned with her ex-husband in Guangzhou. Though Allen has emptied part of the closet for her, most of her things are still packed in the two suitcases she brought from China three months ago, now stacked on top of each other in her side of the closet. In Allen's side, on the shelf above his hanging clothes, he stores his gun collection, which includes a rifle, a shotgun, and a pistol. He lets her use the pistol when he takes her to target shooting on Saturday mornings. The first time she held the exotic weight of a real gun, aiming the pistol at the center of the target, using her dominant eye as instructed by Allen, the black dot enlarging, pulsating, and as she pulled the trigger, the bullet making its inevitable trajectory and her body jerking with the recoil, she was struck by a brand-new thought: she could be anyone in America, even one of those *Kill Bill* girls, fearless, assured, capable of vengeance.

She takes a final glance before stepping into their unit entrance. Allen will not be home for another hour. She gulps down a glass of water in the kitchen and slumps into the green armchair by the living room window. She found the chair by the dumpster, and Allen helped to haul it home. Besides a few bald patches in its upholstery, it's in decent shape and, above all, it feels to be something that's hers.

·

At dinner, Yun tells Allen as best her English allows about the man at the library. Allen puts down his fork, looks at her with an expression she has seen a few times before—when he was filling out her immigration papers or when he saw something on the news—a tightening of lips, bunching of brows. "Chinese women *are* different from American women," he says. "If it was an American woman, she would just say *no* to the guy, say I'm not interested."

"But how do I say no? He asked to sit down at the desk. It's public desk. I thought it's rude—"

"Well, an American woman would say *no* if the guy made her uncomfortable."

He goes to the living room and turns on the TV. She cleans the dishes. When she was a teenager in China, a hand grabbed her breast in a crowded bus. She was too startled or ashamed to make a sound. All she could do was to glance at the man's face—which was blank as if it had nothing to do with the groping hand—and elbow her way out of his reach. She vowed she would slap whoever dared to do that to her again. But she had never slapped anyone's face. When her ex told her that he needed a child of his own after all, she did not even think of slapping him until he was gone.

•

After the divorce, she became invisible. Men would look right through her at someone younger, prettier. On TV, an interracial couple was interviewed: the Chinese woman looked older than her, holding a Chinese child on her lap; the man wore a grayish blond goatee and a comfortable smile. They met on the internet, the woman said, fell in love, got married, and came back here to adopt the child. We're happy, she concluded, and her husband repeated her last words in Chinese with a delicious accent.

Yun's first overseas dates ended quickly. They asked to Skype as soon as the emailing began. She signed up for a course at the Crazy English center. She had seen it advertised on TV: hundreds of people stood on a rooftop or in an open field or an outdoor stadium, shouting out English words in unison. It looked ludicrous but also oddly alluring. During her trial class, she got a bonus—with the yelling out of each word, however it was pronounced, whatever it meant, her interior became less tangled, as though each word, each sound, foreign as it was, was able to loosen the knots inside her bit by bit. After each session, her feet felt lighter on the pavement, her stomach less knobby, and she was more ready to move forward from emails to audio and video communication. And the idea of overseas marriage felt less crazy.

Allen "winked" at her. On his profile: forty-eight, Caucasian, a tech company employee, divorced without children, and in the blank under "Wanting Children or Not," he put "Not sure." She put the same. Allen said the reason for his divorce was that his wife had cheated on him. She said the same. Neither pushed for details. Neither was too interested in Skype either. On the phone, Allen's voice sounded titillatingly foreign, his English exotic, authentic, unlike the yelling Crazy English, which had started to feel like some remote version of Chinese. He told her he liked science fiction and she got hold of some of the movies on pirated DVDs, watching them diligently as if taking an independent study.

The first time she saw him in person, at the Guangzhou Baiyun Airport, he did not recognize her right away. She had not pushed to the very front of the pickup crowd, and when he came out of the exit, a head taller than many of the homebound travelers, she raised her arm to wave at him, but his eyes swept right across her and stopped at a younger woman standing by the exit. A smiley exchange followed between them and she suddenly wasn't sure whether he was Allen or not. She had seen a dozen photos of him, but realized now that she was never quite sure what he looked like. His face seemed to shift from photo to photo, and when at night she imagined his body pressing hers, his face remained blurry.

The man who might or might not be Allen looked up from the younger woman and glanced again across the crowd, his eyes uneasy now. She waved again, this time standing on her toes to be taller. He saw her, wove his way through the crowd toward her, and, when they were a foot apart, raised a brow. "Yun?" he said her name in his peculiar way. She nodded. He gave her a full-body hug; she giggled girlishly. Nobody had paid her much attention earlier, but now they looked at her with gaping mouths. She took hold of Allen's hand, guiding him out of the crowd, as though any moment these people might do something to her—to them.

That night when they made love, he put her on top of him, her flat belly on his bulky one. His pale flesh spread. He grabbed her hips and moved her up and down upon him, like she was a pump, but it was her belly that was filled with air.

•

The next day at the library Yun finds a study area on the second floor: a row of single desks between the windows and tall shelves. She picks an empty desk blocked out of view from the stair landing.

Around mid-afternoon, when she turns to the window to rest her eyes, she sees the man. He is marching down the sidewalk toward the library, his body straight, pace determined and methodic like those Terminators in the movies. The GRE words swirl. She copies more: *pestilence, petrify, petulant* . . . When she looks up, he is there, striding toward her down the narrow aisle between the desks and the shelves, a self-congratulatory glimmer in his eyes. She holds her breath as he brushes past.

When she looks up again, it takes a chilling second

to discern something shadowy behind a crack between books—an eye, his eye, leveling its gaze on her like a gun muzzle. She drops her head like someone condemned. A few seconds later, when she's able to lift her eyes again, he is no longer there, the crack a tiny vacuum.

She stuffs her things in her backpack and scampers out of the library. She glances behind her several times, the hair on her back standing up, as if there is an icy finger touching her. When she reaches home, she hooks the security latch after locking the door.

She is making dinner when the knob turns, followed by a push and straining of the latch. She crosses the living room in hesitant steps. "Allen?" "Yes!" Of course it's Allen, but as she unhooks the latch, she can't shed the vision of the strange man's fervid and oddly impersonal eyes. She would try to shut the door back up, leaning all her weight against it, but he would have already thrust a sturdy foot in.

"Looks like you've got a stalker," Allen says after she describes the new development—even more haltingly than last night. He interrupts her several times with "Slow down, you're not making sense," and in her apologetic attempt to rephrase, reword, repronounce, her more pressing sense of linguistic incompetence dulls her terror a little.

"What's a stalker?" she asks.

"It is someone who stalks you, follows you around." He

stands by the kitchen door, eying her. "Surely you have stalkers in China."

She puts down the spatula, finds her electronic dictionary in the living room, asks him to spell the word, and types it in. She sees no simple equivalent of the word: its translation reads very much like a Chinese rendering of what Allen has just said. Oftentimes when she learns a new English word that refers to a known thing, she feels a small satisfaction, like another loose piece has just found its rightful place in a never-ending jigsaw puzzle. But this word only confirms the man's criminality and her own victimhood—only months in America, still waiting for her work permit, she has become a target of a *stalker*, something that doesn't even have a word in Chinese.

"What do you do with a stalker?"

"I don't know. I've never been stalked . . . Maybe don't dress like a twenty-year-old?"

She's wearing jeans and a gray t-shirt, purposefully picked for today to be anonymous. Yesterday, she wore a pencil skirt and a V-neck top that showed a bit of cleavage, and her skin felt plucked under the man's peeking eyes. "I don't, I don't dress different from other women my age, American women or Chinese women!"

"Well, if you say so." Allen loosens his lips. "Asian women look younger than their age anyway."

He steps over to give her a hug. She resists the urge to recoil from him, his large frame, his musky smell she holds her breath against.

•

She stays at home the next day, a Friday, slumped in her green armchair, a GRE book on her lap.

She misses Crazy English, the yelling, the camaraderie, the collective visions for a future floating above everyone's head like auspicious clouds. The mouths shaped around those potent syllables as though they must contain all that was missing here and now. No one wanted to believe those hardship stories: "Tell You a Real America," "A Chinese Immigrant's Real Experience in America," "A Chinese Woman's Real Account of Her Transnational Marriage." No one cared about those so-called "Reals," which were not what kept their voices sonorant and buoyant in Guangzhou's smoggy air.

She rises from her chair, steps to the center of the living room, and starts yelling out words the way she did at the center: *phan-tom, phi-lan-thro-py, phleg-ma-tic, pi-geon-hole* . . . The syllables bounce against the shaded window, the security-latched door, the bare wall, Allen's plywood shelf loaded with science fiction books and DVDs, his multi-drawer desk holding his computer, soup-can pen-holder, insulated coffee mug, and a book with a spaceship on the cover, his swivel office chair, his faux-leather couch with the visible dent on the side where he always sits, and the glass-topped coffee table with his bonsai tree placed exactly at the center. "This little tree belongs here," he said once when she moved it aside to clean the table and forgot to move it back. "It gets the exact right amount of sunlight where I put it." He cares for it as though it were his infant child, watering it with a measuring cup, misting its miniature leaves, trimming its branches like they were tiny fingernails. And she loves him for that. She must, she tells herself, as the odd syllables fall like crumbs around her.

·

After dinner, Allen drives her to the bookstore. It is part of the routine—bookstore on Friday nights.

She sees him right way—sitting alone at a table in the café, holding a magazine while eyeing two women at a nearby table—both of them Asian, maybe Chinese, maybe Korean or Vietnamese. She grips Allen's arm to stop him on his way to the café where he will order a grande mocha and take a seat. "That man," she whispers, "the stalker."

Allen pauses. The man turns his head toward them.

She cringes, cowering beside Allen. Allen steps onto the escalator, she trails along. "I still don't know which one you were pointing at," he says at the second-floor landing, looking lost for a moment before heading toward the science fiction shelf.

"The one in the striped shirt," she whispers, "gray hair, young face, maybe my age, maybe not, I can't tell."

Allen makes no comment, removing a book from the shelf. They are standing between two shelves, out of sight from the escalator landing.

"He stares at two women, Asian—" Her voice breaks off: the man is standing right there in the aisle, cocking his head at her, squinting as if to make sure she is what he thinks, then walks on.

"It's him—" She elbows Allen, mouthing the words.

Allen looks at the empty aisle. She knows any moment the man will be circling back, or maybe he is peeping through a crack at her right now.

"I'll tell the manager someone's following my wife," Allen says after they back away from the shelves to the stair landing.

"What will they do?" she asks, still whispering. "Will they catch him?"

Allen does not respond. He steps down the escalator; she follows him. He heads over to the café instead of the customer service desk. Had he decided not to tell the manager then? Let's go home, she wants to say, but she doesn't really want to go home—it's their night out, a weekly treat. Allen gets his mocha; she gets a hot tea. They sit down at an empty table. Allen takes out the spaceship book. She takes out her GRE book. After reading for several minutes, Allen stands up, saying, "I'm going to check out some books," and leaves. Her eyes follow him like those of a drowning person. Then she glances across the bookstore—all the shelves seem to grow eyes. She buries her face in the GRE book: *pinnacle, pique, piteous* . . .

When she looks up again, she already knows what she'll see, but still, it appalls her to know how close the man is, how fast and quiet he is able to move, and how settled he appears in his chair, holding a magazine just below his eye level. She buries her face lower in her book and continues to copy.

Allen comes back, putting a new hardcover on the table. The stalker sizes him up before sensing her gaze. His face flushes, his eyes flitting behind his magazine. She nudges Allen on the elbow, pointing her chin at the man. "Can we go?" she mouths the words.

The man is still pretending to read. Allen gets up finally, grabbing his half-finished mocha.

"You can't just walk away whenever there's a problem,"

he says after they get in his car. "Here in America, people face their problems and try to solve them."

"But you're—" Her voice comes out with an edge but falls silent. She swallows the words "my husband." What does she expect from a husband? The old one left just like that and is now more distant than a stranger. The new one, in a way, still feels like a stranger. The night air suddenly turns to the color of a nasty bruise. Buildings are dark or dimly lit: What's going on inside them? She has no way to know.

"What do you want to do now?" He gives her a long look. "Go home and watch a movie?"

She nods.

•

Saturday morning, at the shooting range, Yun half expects to see the stalker again: omnipresent as he seems.

When she aims Allen's pistol at the target, she sees the stalker looming out of the shadowy shelves, enlarging as he stomps toward her. Cold sweat loosens her grip; she wipes her hands on her jeans: she sees herself crouching like a terrified woman in the movies, muttering the trembling English phrase "Stop or I'll shoot." But he will keep coming, with those evasive eyes and blushing cheeks so mismatched with his body's surety.

She pulls the trigger. A moment of blindness. The bullet goes through the bottom edge of the target.

She aims again, steadying her arms. She exhales. The bullet hits closer to the center, maybe close enough to render an attacker immobile. "Not bad," Allen says, patting her shoulder.

Back in their apartment, she watches Allen clean his guns. She asked him once about this hobby of his, which he had not mentioned during their email exchange, and he said something about one needing to be ready to protect oneself, which she found alarming, but like with many other things she found alarming, she's put it aside to deal with more pressing issues of her new life.

"Why lock them?" she asks as he places the guns in their individual cases.

"Because I don't want them stolen. This isn't a bad neighborhood, but there're still break-ins."

"Can I have a key to the pistol? If there is a break-in and I'm here, alone?"

He doesn't respond right away. Slowly, he puts the pistol in the foamed indent of its case, fastens the lock, and places it on the top shelf in his side of the closet. Then, finally, he goes to the safe squatting at the corner by his side of the bed, turns the combination lock this way and that. He opens it a crack, takes out a key chain, removes one key, and locks it back up. "Make sure you don't lose it." He hands her the key, looking into her eyes like a parent handing down an heirloom.

·

She is still at the letter *p* and her GRE exam is less than a month away. She will fail it, end up waitressing in a Chinese buffet or bagging groceries in an Asian market, fabricating lies to her family and friends on the phone. She cannot go back either, not even if she could bear the shame—her copyediting job was filled less than a week after she turned in her resignation, by a younger woman with a master's degree. Every decent job requires a master's degree now, here or there.

She rises, crosses to the bedroom, and reaches for the pistol case in the closet. After opening it with the key, she holds the gun with both hands and aims it at her reflection in the wall mirror. She stares at her face until it stills. Then she puts the pistol in her purse. It hits her hip as she walks to the library.

It's a newly renovated library with vaulted ceilings and full-length windows. When Allen first took her here, she was elated to know that she didn't have to sit in her green chair in the apartment all day long; she could come here and be around people and actually *feel* she was in America.

She glances across the shelves, aisles, tables, and computer stations. She climbs upstairs, comes to an open study area close to the stair landing, away from the shelves: she would rather that he stare at her in the open than peeping through a hole. She sits by a window, turning her face sideways so that she won't be easily distracted. She copies words in her notebook, the pistol's weight pressing against her lap.

Her eyes are drawn up by the same hunch that has become familiar—he is sitting at a desk two rows diagonally to her left, settled into his magazine-holding, eye-peeking pose. A briefcase leans against his chair. What is in there? Rope, tape, cutting tools, suffocating devices, a pistol?

Her fingers tighten around her purse, feeling the comforting contour of the pistol. From the corner of her eye, she sees him stand up and disappear in the direction behind her, and the space she can't see instantly turns murky.

She stiffens. He strides past her, nearly scraping her elbow, and stops at the desk right in front of her, which, to her dismay, is now empty. Has he just willed away the drowsy man with glasses slipping down his nose? He sits down, holds up the same magazine, his eyes burrowing toward her from behind the crisp pages, latching onto her and patiently, meticulously clawing, chewing her. She looks down at her notebook: *predicament, predilection, prefigure* . . . What do they mean? What do any of these words mean? And after *p*, there are still *q*, *r*, *s*, and *t* . . . "What are you doing!" she hears herself say.

The man shoves the magazine up to cover his face. People turn to look at her.

"He follows me," she explains to the closest pair of eyes, which belong to a woman with a pale, ruffled face, who has been reading at the desk to her left since she got here—surely she has noticed the man peeking at her and closing in on her and will agree those are not normal behaviors. She points at the man who by now has lowered his magazine to his desk and is gazing at her with the same quizzical and indifferent look as everyone else.

The woman shakes her head: "What did you say?"

Yun rises, crossing the three steps to the man's desk. "Why you follow me? What you want from me?" she shouts at him. His clean-shaven face looks innocuously bare, his sprayed grayish hair like trampled wintry grass. He blinks.

"What? What did you say?" His voice comes out steady, not quite as quivery as she remembers.

"You follow me. You stared behind the shelf, like a gun. A pistol. In the bookstore too. You pretend. You stare at me, scare me. You are everywhere!" she yells. She is shaking. Words boom in her lungs, bounce off her vocal cords: they do not feel foreign or stiff, but real, lived. "Why? What you want from me?"

"I don't understand you at all," the man says measuredly.

"You sat down at that desk . . ." She turns to point at the desk downstairs, but her vision is blocked by eyes around her, staring eyes that pin her to where she is, and among the suspended motions and loud murmurs, a man in a dark uniform is striding toward her, his hand resting by his waistline, on top of something resembling a holster, and she becomes aware of her hand, which has not loosened its grip on her pistol-filled purse.

"What's the matter?" the security guard asks, looking at her face like detecting symptoms of madness.

The floor wobbles beneath her, the air buzzes, and Yun suddenly realizes there is something she hasn't yet said to the man—the word *no*. Such an easy syllable to pronounce. So unmistakable it must sound. "No," she summons her strength and says to the stalker, while knowing how ineffectual it can be.

SUN AND MOON

There is a fertility rock on the northern shore of Pagsum Lake, a few hundred kilometers east of Lhasa. Lanlan reads online that the rock is shaped like a woman's vulva, with all the lips, creases, and clefts in the right place, amplified multiple times, smooth to the touch like female skin. Women from far and near travel there to pray for a child.

Lanlan had a miscarriage due to "abnormal" uterine lining—according to the diagnosis of the specialist who wore one strand of hair wrapped around his bald crown. Groping his hair to ensure it was in place, he asked her if she'd had an abortion before. She answered no, but he continued as if he did not hear her, "Some young women think they can abort their children as freely as they want, but everything has consequences."

"I've never had an abortion before," Lanlan said again, her face flushing, which she knew could be taken as a sign of deception. Her husband Li Qiang was looking at her, his eyes already skeptical. The doctor turned to him. "Either way," he said, "your wife's uterine lining is *abnormal*. I'm afraid she will have another miscarriage if you try again."

•

When she hit thirty, Lanlan suddenly wanted a child. She wanted it badly. And she approached her desire methodically—calculating her ovulation, measuring her temperature, and, asking Li Qiang to do it for her, she phrased her request like a threat: I don't think our marriage can go on without a child. He looked thoughtful, as if he was considering what this would mean for him, what he had to lose or gain from it. Maybe he wanted to be a parent too. Maybe he dreamed of a son who would not be like him, the way she dreamed of a daughter who would live a different life from hers.

Lanlan was fifteen when it happened—in a wild date grove on the hill by the railway that cut through the middle of her small hometown, Luzhen, which was known for nothing but spicy dry tofu. The grove was said to be haunted and Lanlan had gone there before, with the same neighborhood boy, when she was younger. They had waited until dusk to see if the rumored ghost fire would rise above the rugged gravestones that were scattered among trees and weeds. They had held hands when they ran down the hill screaming at the first glance of a possible blue glimmer.

She had known the boy since kindergarten, and that year, when they both turned fifteen, he hit a growth spurt: his hands, in particular, seemed to have doubled their size. She couldn't help but stare at them. When he said he wanted to show her something in the grove, she thought he would show her the real ghost fire, or more probably, he would confess to her that he liked her. She wasn't in love with him, but she felt lonely and wanted something. As they climbed side by side up the hill, she wondered what it would be like to hold his alarmingly big hand. He was quiet. She pressed him to tell her what he wanted to show her. He said she would find out soon. He tried to smile, but his face looked dark. She was suddenly afraid. When they came to a clearing where the two other boys each sat on a tombstone, she thought they were ghosts at first. The next moment, the boy's large hand was on her mouth. When they pushed her down, the train rumbled past, and the ground beneath her shook and shook.

•

She told Li Qiang nothing about it. Regarding her past romance, she told him this: She had one boyfriend before him, a boy she had first seen when riding her bicycle to school, who, about halfway, would appear from the opposite direction riding his bicycle to another school. Then, one day, he was waiting for her in front of her school gate. But it didn't work out: they got into different colleges and eventually grew apart.

The night after the doctor's visit, she extended that version, sharing with him a piece of truth minus everything leading up to it. She told him about the crusty-eyed doctor whom she found by dialing a number scribbled on an electric pole. The man wore a reassuring white lab coat and mask, but the room reminded her of a public toilet, with its faint stench and unpainted walls and ceiling. Anyway, she told Li Qiang, it hurt so much that she thought she would die there and then.

They were lying in bed. Li Qiang reached out and touched her hand. She moved closer to him, but he put a knee in between them, even though he continued to stroke her hand. "It's okay if we don't have a child of our own," he said. "We can adopt. Or we can just live the way we were."

She could see what it would be like to live the way they were: Li Qiang would be out with his "buddy" Ah Lun five nights a week, claiming they were playing badminton in the gym; she would debate with herself whether to track them down and catch them in bed somewhere. And feel cheated, stupid. But then what?

•

On the computer screen, the fertility rock looks small, shadowy, contoured with two white khatas to highlight the stone vulva. Otherwise, most people probably wouldn't look at it twice. But it does have those embarrassing pleats once Lanlan enlarges the photo.

On her first day in Lhasa, after checking into a fly-in-fested hotel, Lanlan gets on a rickshaw to the Potala Palace, which was in her view for most part of her minibus ride from the airport—first from afar like a painted rock formation on the mountaintop, then this magnificent palace pulling pilgrims in woolen chuba toward it. Now she rides past them as they spin prayer wheels and mutter mantras. Some prostrate after each step forward, their foreheads callused, long braids dusty.

After the driver lets her off in front of the stairs leading up to the palace, a weight suddenly drops in her head and legs, which she figures a moment later must be the altitude sickness. She sits down on the curb before dizziness can trip her and rests her head on her knees. She laughs quietly to herself. Here she is: in front of the highest palace in the world but hardly able to move. The sun pours out. People swirl. She feels calm somehow, like the eye of a storm.

She thinks of herself as a survivor. She has managed to get into a college and away from her town. She has dated, made advances, and each time as she climbed onto another boy, she wanted to feel a salvation. She would not lie down, not allow them to ride her. But it did not take much, a glint in the eyes, a grunt in the throat, to make it all come back again.

Li Qiang is different. When occasionally he does have sex with her, at her request, he enters her from behind. Sometimes she rides him, in the dark. They never keep the light on. She never has to ask for that. He is gentle, incapable of doing the kind of things the three boys had done to her. She feels safe with him, if not dishonest. Sometimes she wonders how he and Ah Lun do it. She is sure they've been doing it—maybe they are in their bed right now. But he's not going to give her a divorce. She has asked, yelled, and they've wept together. He wraps his arm around her when they have company. While at night, in bed, they continue to lie on opposite ends like two question marks.

Maybe she can continue to live like this if she has a child, a daughter, to be specific—while everyone else wants a son, she wants a daughter. She will not allow what happened to her to happen to her daughter. She will be a good mother, present, unlike her own mother, who had made it clear that she'd wished her to be a son the moment she was born. And who had paid thousands of yuan in fines just to eventually have one. That was why Lanlan couldn't tell her mother anything. She was on her own. Has always been.

Lanlan sits on the curb until the sun sinks and cold rises from the ground. She shivers, raises an arm to a rickshaw driver, and asks him to take her to the nearest hospital. There, she is given a rubber bag pumped full of oxygen. She lies down on a cot, holding the bag like a float, and inhales.

•

She wakes up the next morning to the buzzing of flies, each green-headed and ferocious. It takes her a moment to remember where she is and what she is doing here. The fertility rock. But it seems rather ridiculous now to take a four-hour bus ride just to go see a rock. A rock is a rock, no matter how it is shaped. The power of faith seems flimsy with her lingering headache and the black flies spinning above her, chanting their tireless *I want, I want.*

Instead, she comes to the Potala Palace again,

determined to climb up the stairs this time. Entering the gate, she sees a young lama seated on a stool by the corridor wall, scribbling something in a notebook. In a saffron robe with one shoulder bare, he has the pronounced Tibetan brown complexion and angular nose and chin. He is very young, perhaps not yet twenty. On his shaven head, new black hair seems to be pushing out this very second. He looks up.

"What are you writing?" she asks.

"A love letter," he says.

"To a nun?" she says and quickly laughs.

He is a resident lama who works part-time as a tour guide. His name is Dhargey, which, he tells her, means *progress, development, spreading*. He gives her a tour around the murals and statues, amid thousands of flickering flames of yak-butter lamps that look like thousands of miniature sunsets.

In one of the galleries, she sees a row of bronze statuettes with naked female figures mounted on the laps of naked male figures who sit cross-legged on lotus thrones. Some of the males have spokes of arms. Some wear crowns of skulls. Some twine their arms around their female partners' gleaming torsos. The females' faces are hidden or seen only in profile, with tongues extending toward the males' mouths.

"They're yab-yum, symbolizing the union of compassion and insight," says Dhargey in a matter-of-fact voice. "The male deity represents compassion; the female represents insight; their union, enlightenment."

Lanlan tries to keep her face neutral. But in her head, she sees two faceless bodies of flesh, not bronze, looped around each other in the yab-yum position, fusing, igniting. She sees her rickety bed in the fly-swarming hotel room. A vision clearly wrong.

The yak-butter lamps leap and tremble, like heartbeats in flame, burning away dimness however small.

That night, lying in her hotel bed, she imagines sitting on Dhargey's lap, in the yab-yum position. She will feel him harden, feel the urge to move, to pull. Do the male and female deities not feel pleasure fused in that position? Do they not think of a child, a physical one, instead of, or in addition to, metaphysical enlightenment?

But she will just have another miscarriage, maybe again at work, like last time, inside a restroom stall: the cramps, the gray sac the size of a Ping-Pong ball bobbing among dark blood and clots in the toilet bowl. It was a relief not being able to see through the blood and mucus to what curled inside.

·

The fertility rock stands on a pile of erratically shaped rocks. It's about the size of an adult head. She wishes it were larger, more grandiose, something one could look up at like a monument. The size of a door, perhaps, that would allow an adult to pass through. Tourists are taking photos in front of it, joking, giggling. Lanlan stands away from them. The only person praying is a Tibetan woman who is about Lanlan's age, her palms closed, eyes closed, her forehead lowered to her fingertips.

Lanlan waits until the tourists trickle away. Then she closes her eyes and puts her palms in front of her chest like the Tibetan woman.

If it is possible to backtrack. If she had not gone to the date grove with the boy with big hands, whom she had to see again and again at school and in the neighborhood, as her body raged inside. If she had said hi to the boy on the bicycle a day earlier, had waited for him at his school gate, the way she imagined he'd do for her.

But it could have been worse. They could have killed her, the three boys who are now in their thirties like her, living their lives in that same old town, raising children as though nothing had happened. Or the bogus doctor who held the thing up in his gloved hand like holding a half-pound meat at the grocery. She had covered her face, believing he would toss it at her the next moment.

She opens her eyes and looks at the earth mother's stone vulva—its lips and creases ossified, bearing no exit or entrance.

She dozes off on the bus ride back to Lhasa. She is inside the rock, in a dark purple pool of water, with the Tibetan woman. Both of them have shrunk to the size of an infant, but they look just the same, with wrinkles starting to line their faces, and eyes wavering but fiery. The woman says something to her in Tibetan, and then swims toward what appears to be an island in the center of the water. Lanlan does not understand her but follows anyway. It is actually a tree. She sees as she swims closer, a floating banyan tree.

The woman holds on to a dangling root and looks up. Lanlan swims to her side and does the same. She sees children of different ages and sizes swing among its branches, its aerial roots tied at the end where they sit and swing. They look all right in their perpetual swinging, like planets orbiting.

But then Lanlan sees these children's eyes. They are not blinking. Their faces are equally blank. They make no sound. Even their legs are not moving. The aerial roots are swinging by themselves. And there is no light. The tree grows in the dimness, upon whatever life is left in these children.

The Tibetan woman reaches out to a little girl near her. It seems she is trying to stop the child from the swinging, to hold her and rock her back to life.

•

During the next few days, Lanlan wanders around the city, this holy land where tourists like her are all looking for something. They are like her, she thinks, giving away change to vagrants on the streets, as they would not do in their own cities, where they have become callous at their sight. They are recovering a better self, trying to be closer to the Buddha-nature.

There are many vagrants. Many look like they've traveled from far-off mountains and prairies, wearing thick chuba, carrying their few belongings in woolen bundles. Many are with small children, who have a peculiar way of gazing at you, their dark eyes severe, unblinking. They make Lanlan remember her dream and the children swinging in the tree. She seemed to have seen herself there too, her fifteen-year-old self swinging among those children, though she had not remembered herself to look that young at fifteen.

One morning, while eating a steamed bun from a street vendor, Lanlan is startled to see a child standing right by her, gazing up at her face without a sound. She stops chewing. She looks around and sees a woman watching them from a dozen meters away. Lanlan buys two more buns and places them in the child's hands. The child runs to his mother, who smiles and nods at her. Lanlan smiles and nods back. She feels good for a moment, and then she feels sorry, so sorry she wants to hold on to the mother and child and cry.

At night, lying on her hotel bed, she imagines not going back to her low-altitude city, which is like a dust-bowl, and she, a particle of dust blown back and forth from home to work, work to home. Instead of going back to that threadbare life, she will withdraw all her money from her bank, give it away, and then she will be one of them, hun-kered on the roadside in tatters, her empty palms held out in the sun, begging from those who have wronged or been wronged elsewhere in the world.

"Here, keep this." They will hand her a dirty, wrinkled one-yuan bill. And she will take it as though she is giving them a blessing.

·

The day before her departure, Lanlan returns to the Potala Palace. She stands again in front of the largest Buddha statue in the central hall. She has stood in front of many Buddha statues by now. They are everywhere: the low-cast eyes, the full, round face. She has felt her heart rattle but does not know if it is real, or if it's only what she's supposed to feel, standing below the immense, soft eyes that seem to care about you and know what you have been through and tell you it's okay. You are still loved. I feel your pain, because I saw it. When it happened, I saw everything.

Dhargey is giving a tour to a foreign woman, his English accented but comfortable, like his Mandarin. The auburn-haired woman nods and touches his elbow: she looks a little too eager as she leans her face to him. And Lanlan sees her own self in this woman who has traveled even farther to get here, to look for something or redeem something, and to see a temporary illusion in this young Tibetan boy who has no fault, no dark history, who is supposed to practice emptiness, detachment, and reject the flesh that she and the woman each carry with them.

Lanlan follows them, trying not to be noticed. They come to the yab-yum gallery. Dhargey is now reciting the symbolism of the naked intertwined shiny statuettes in the same matter-of-fact voice. Lanlan can see that he too is trying to keep a neutral face, but his eyes and bare shoulder betray him. He must want, too. How can he not? He must want and want to be wanted. He is ordinarily vain too, enjoying the lone tourist's shy fascination. He must wonder if these women ever imagine getting into that showcased position with him—if only he would let them climb onto him, hold them tight and be the embodiment of compassion, giving his beautiful body to them so that they could obtain enlightenment and carry it back to where they are from. Be whole again.

Lanlan is about to turn away before he sees her. He says something to the other tourist and walks over.

"It's you," he says. Not a question, but a statement, as though he has been expecting her. It could have been what the boy on the bicycle said to her had she waited for him in front of his school gate, or somewhere on his way home, riding into his view.

"Yes, I was looking for you. I want to say goodbye before I leave. Say thank you."

"For what?"

"For showing me around."

"You've thanked me already." He chuckles.

The other woman is waiting for him to come back. Their eyes meet: he is only a boy, they seem to say to each other.

"Formally, take you to dinner. Good-bye dinner," Lanlan says.

•

She waits for Dhargey outside the palace. The sun is slanting but still strong—the sun that loves the bruised, the childless and aging no better or worse. The moon is also in the sky, half-full, transparent, cool, watching her like a distant mother who has finally offered her attention.

Dhargey exits the gate in a navy jacket, blue jeans, and baseball cap. He smiles self-consciously, as though he is not sure what she will think of him in this layman outfit. Whether he has lost some charm or potency without his saffron robe and shaved head. Or maybe he is simply not sure about going out with a tourist woman over ten years older. No matter what it is, Lanlan finds his uncertainty touching, and his youthfulness. The world is malleable right now, overflowing with the sun's amber light and the moon's deep-well one.

They pause on their way to listen to a blind musician strumming a dramyin by the roadside. His sightless eyes seeing what they cannot see. When he stops, his galloping notes make phantom leaps. Light bounces on his quivering strings.

They come to a Tibetan restaurant painted with primary colors and steeped in the salty, creamy scent of yak-butter tea. They order beer and meats, which, she finds out, Dhargey is not forbidden to consume. He can also stay out late from time to time and slip back into the palace through a back door. He even dated a girl not long ago—a Han girl who worked at a hair salon.

The light outside the windows has dimmed, while that inside the restaurant gathers heat and depth. Lanlan wants to touch Dhargey's forehead, the sweat seeping out as he talks about his decision to be a lama. His father had hoped to be a lama before meeting his mother. Since Dhargey was a child, his father had hoped his son would become a lama to fulfill what he himself had failed. He is not going to disappoint his father, Dhargey says.

Lanlan knows he is telling the truth. He doesn't need to lie, unlike herself. She can hear all the lies she has told others, and all the lies she has been told. She hopes that her husband, Li Qiang, and Ah Lun have been making love to each other, and that they will continue to do so. It will not be easy. It won't be easy for anyone. Including Dhargey, who is telling his story of commitment and self-sacrifice. A good, kind story. There is kindness in the world, and it is floating right around her like wispy air. If she shifts her body the right way, or turns her face in the right angle, she may breathe it in and feel her next exhale to be easeful and free. She wants to touch Dhargey the way she has never touched another person before.

Maybe it will be in her squeaky hotel bed, the flies swarming above them like an obscene wreath. No, not there. It should be by the Lhasa River where she has walked alone at dusk. The moon will shed its watery light. The wildness with its rolling mountains, glaciers, shrub lands, and gorges will press in, while the city behind them loses its substance, leaving only the fluttering of prayer flags. They will sit next to each other on the damp grass. The air will be thin and brisk. She will feel chiseled and clean and will climb onto his lap, into the yab-yum position. If he hesitates, opening his mouth to stop her, she will touch his lips and say, "Let me love you. Hold me and let me love."

TO SAY

My grandfather did not say much when he paid a visit to his village family years later. He saw his daughter—awkward, avoiding eye contact, dark-skinned like him and with his straight nose bridge and cleft chin. The resemblance made him uneasy, the kind of uneasiness he felt when he missed a step assembling his rifle back during the wartime and the gun almost misfired, or when his comrade was shot in the chest and he ran away, jabbed by the feeling that he could have saved him. Through the years he thought of him more often than of his village wife, though he dreamt of her drowning once, her feet so small they looked like split fish tails. She was underwater, a blue substance, an outline, but neither scared nor particularly distressed. She looked the way she did when he made love to her those few nights after their wedding, before he joined

the army, her face disquietingly serene, as if she was sacrific-
ing herself, as if she knew it was the beginning and the end.

He had not thought much about their daughter either.
There were letters written by a hired hand informing him
of her birth, the milestones such as first tooth and first
step. He did not write back nor try to imagine what she
looked like. He wished her mother would remarry like a
postwar modern woman, while knowing she could never
be modern: she was illiterate and had feet that could not be
stretched back to their natural size. The world she lived in
could not be renewed, so he had to stay away. Then the ar-
gument would collapse, like the stairs he climbed in sleep
crumbling under his feet. He would step into nothing and
awake to find his new city wife lying by his side.

.

My mother later visited him once, in his house, which
was in a city two hours' train ride from their village. For
the first time she put on the navy blue wool coat he had
given her as a gift. She wanted to say something to him,
on behalf of her mother, who she knew would want to say
something, but couldn't, and instead grew more and more
silent. The words remained tangled and sunken inside her
mother and she wanted to salvage them, to bring them to

light, and let them hang crystal clear in the space between her and her father.

But she could not say anything. Her stepmother offered her some candies as though she were a child. She didn't want any but took one out of politeness. She answered a few questions about her college life and got up, and as she stepped out of their door, she said, once again, thank you for the coat.

·

My grandmother's feet would remain cold, like two snails, remain out of the sun and out of people's sight, until tuberculosis killed her the second year she lived with us. My mother took the train, brought her ash jar to her village, and buried her by her parents. There she was back to her childhood, among wildflowers and wind and other free-growing things.

At the burial mound, my mother found the knots that once lived inside her mother now within her. They must be untangled a little before she could stand up, leave her mother physically behind for good, and take the southbound train to the city where she had settled down, to the life her mother had dreamed up for her: that of a modern, literate woman, of shampoo, tap water, and electricity.

The first day she went to the boarding school twenty miles away from home, which was also the only high school in the area, her mother staggered on her small feet to keep up. In her mind, her mother's feet diminished with each step she took. The two other girls from the village and their father or uncle had outpaced them a long way ahead. She asked her mother to go back so she could catch up with her team. "You're too slow," she might have said, or "I would have been faster without you." And she realized how imprecise, injurious her words could be.

.

In her preverbal stage, my daughter cried so much I thought maybe she had been taken out too soon, not quite ready for the boundless world, or that a phantom in our apartment was haunting her—she would stare at a corner of the ceiling and cry harder, while all I could see were sun speckles and dust motes. Or maybe she was saddened by something, memories of her forebears, the bygone and forgotten temporarily surfacing in her tender brain.

Her cry sounded ancient, like a river that flowed from a far-off place. I remembered the gray crane standing on one leg looking into the river of my hometown, and the next time I saw it, it lay sideways, half buried in sand.

I held my daughter, lost in her cry, and saw my grandmother looking into the river that flowed past her village.
Her face thin, insubstantial, like the crane's but paler. She
was once known for her pale complexion, as it was rare in
her village of tanned farmers. She would sit there by the
river during her morning sickness. Something moved in the
waves, tugging at her knotted stomach. She saw knots everywhere: nests in the trees, last winter's vines amid new growth,
waterweeds flushed up the bank by moon-drawn tides.

With a stick, she drew in the sand, a circle, a door, a
face. She drew pictures, inventing words for herself. When
she wanted to draw her feelings, she drew knots overlapping knots. Then she cupped some water with her hands
and poured it over her drawings.

Her daughter, my mother, stirred, bubbled, rising up,
a little goldfish in a water tank. He may come back, my
grandmother thought, just in time for the birth. She pic-
tured my grandfather holding a rifle that she had seen the
recruiter carry on one shoulder. The neat green uniform
cinched at the waist with a buckled belt.

.

My grandmother did not say much during the year she
lived with us, the last year of her life—not to my mother,

nor to me, nor to the few older folks in the neighborhood she occasionally sat with in the sun. What words were turning inside her, as she cooked, waited for us to come home from work, from school, as she ate, slept? Words that surged forth, subsided, surged forth again. They birthed, they died, consumed and renewed each other, bred and multiplied. They made her head heavy. She bent her head, like the lean locust tree in front of our window, its leaves rustling until they were gone.

·

When my daughter turned one, I took her on her first cross-ocean flight to visit my family. I thought of those Russian dolls—how comforting it would be to be held by a larger pair of arms and rest awhile like my child. But my mother had grown even shorter and thinner than I. She looked frail holding my rosy, robust daughter in her arms. Neither of us had a larger pair of arms to hold the other two.

Before leaving again, I asked her to tell me about my grandmother. She looked away. "What's there to tell?" she said. "She lived a hard life and died not yet sixty."

·

If my grandmother did like to draw, what would she draw? As she sat on a rock by the river flowing past her village, having finished laundry, what pictograms or ideograms would she invent for herself? What words that she could not say would she draw out in the sand to be later erased by water and wind?

Would she draw my grandfather's warm adolescent face bent over to hers on their wedding night, his awkward goodbye smile a month later, his absorption in the person he would become, his transformation and her stillness? Would she, at the end of her drawing, draw a large hand that was larger than everything else she had drawn? A hand that put her here and him there, put a rifle in his hand and a stick in hers, a hand neither he nor she could see, but which exerted its pressure on them at any moment. The drawing made her feel as if he was a child she knew only briefly before he was sent away, to outside the village gate, and he had to keep walking until the yellow plain looked directionless. Until the crooked old tree she leaned against became an emaciated guardian for a life he couldn't return to.

·

My mother took me to visit my grandfather once, a few years after my grandmother died, in his house in that northern city not too far from her home village. He looked at me briefly and looked away. He had a serious face, like my mother's, and they had the same straight nose bridge and cleft chin. The resemblance made me uneasy. I wanted to look at him but did not want him to notice I was looking. My step-grandmother was a plump woman with short, permed hair and a pinched smile. She kept offering us candies and did most of the talking.

But try as she might, we sat mostly in silence, or at least that was how I remembered that visit. Words might be turning inside each of us, but we kept our tongues arrested. Our eyes glanced around one another but were also turned to something absent, someone who was not there. We sat as though in mourning. Maybe that was why my mother took me there—maybe the silence, rather than unsaid words, was what she carried inside her—so that the three of us, for the first and only time, could gather together, brief as it was, and mourn for my grandmother.

•

Later, in my twenties, before I went abroad, my mother gave me the navy blue coat. It looked barely worn, out of fashion, its blue had faded along the folds, and it smelled of mothballs and decades-old wool. I kept it in my suitcase until one cold winter, the kind when branches were locked in ice, cracking all around you, as though to echo and magnify some inner breaking you alone could hear. I put the coat on for the first time. It was heavy, mute, but kept me warm.

SIGNS

Cangjie, who has four eyes, is a record keeper in the court of the Yellow Emperor (2698–2598 B.C.). Like his predecessors, he ties knots of different styles, sizes, and colors to record wars, ceremonies, tribal populations, food allocations, and other affairs. But as events diversify and multiply and knots accumulate, sorting them out, tying more, remembering what each stands for, becomes too difficult a task.

"Create a new record-keeping system then," the emperor commands him. "Let each sign be unique. Create and teach it to other people, so all shall know what a sign represents."

Cangjie falls asleep thinking. He sees a wrinkled face—his dead mother's face, on which he discerns a pattern, a sort of blueprint. As he looks closer at each given detail, more details emerge and each seems to be pointing at something—a tree, a river, a bridge, a man ploughing, a woman sewing, a baby asleep . . . They must be the signs he is seeking. If he can copy them down before the dream breaks, his job of creating a new mnemonic system will be complete. But he cannot find a sandy or rocky surface to draw them on or carve them in. He tries to memorize them, to press them into his brain.

When he wakes up, the signs that appeared so lucid in his dream blur. He steps out of his house and looks around—the fields, the hills, the cows, the deer, the rising sun. To think a set of signs can represent them seems once again an illusion.

He tries to recall the signs that appeared on his mother's face but knows that whatever still lingers in his memory are but approximations. His mother's face has gone back to the elements of the world, the signs back to their origins.

•

Cangjie goes to the court. Standing at the doorway of the Record Room, he looks at the knotted ropes hanging down from the low ceiling. With a hand, he brushes across the ropes close to him: they dangle and dance in his four eyes and he sees their colors fade, the knots loosen, the braided strands disintegrate like buried hair.

He steps toward the back of the room and stops in front of a red knot tied like a noose and dyed with bloodroot. It represents the Battle of Zhuolu, fought between the Yellow Emperor and Chiyou, leader of the nine eastern tribes, over the Yellow River's fertile valley. The war broke out in the year of Cangjie's birth. His father was enlisted that year and never came back. He remembers his father's face hovered above him, his eyes shivering with something that made Cangjie cry. His mother scooped him up, pressed his face to her chest.

A couple rows to its left hangs a gray tangle of knots shaped like a hornet nest—the Season of Wolves. His mother was working in the field, carrying him in a sling on her back, when he started screaming, "Big dogs, many, many big dogs!" He pointed his fingers to the woods. Though all she could see were shadowy branches, she knew what her son saw were wolves, a word she had not yet taught him. "Wolves coming!" she called out to the villagers as she started running. When they reached their door, a dozen wolves leapt out of the woods like a tidal wave. His mother told him this story one day when, in a pail of water, he saw his own reflection and suddenly understood why people stared for a long time at his face, why bigger kids called him "little monster," and why he saw the shiver in his father's eyes.

Two more rows down to the left is a rope of stopper knots colored pallid white—the Year of Drought. His mother knelt on the roadside of the marketplace, holding him with one arm, holding her hand out to passersby: "Hungry. Pity my child." She held his face to her chest so that he would not see—except that he did. He saw people avert their eyes, many also with moaning stomachs. His mother still nursed him, but her milk would quickly dribble to a stop. He feared that he would suck her dry and she would droop like the wheat stalks on their small plot of land. He saw an old lady—so old her hair bun was the size of a snail—stagger toward them, grab a handful of soybeans from her bowl and gingerly put them in his mother's hand.

·

That night, he puts a turtle shell by his bed and a carving knife next to it, and then he closes his eyes. If his mother's face reappears in his dream, he will try to open his upper pair of eyes and carve those signs on the turtle shell. He will keep his lower pair closed and gazing inward at his mother's face until he has inscribed all the signs.

But instead of his mother's face, he sees the winding path lined with hawthorn hedges behind his house. It leads to the poplar woods, and there, at the trailhead, his mother sits on her heels on the ground.

"Mother," he calls as he kneels down by her and holds her hands in his—they are small and bony like two hollowed birds.

She turns her face toward him, her eyes cloudy, but he knows she can see him—she can see him as a baby who cried incessantly because the world was vast with too many unknowable things, and as a young man telling her that he was selected to be the court record keeper, and as he is now in his middle age, hair and beard graying, assigned by the emperor the impossible task of inventing a system of signs.

"Child," his mother says, "signs are everywhere. You will see them as you've seen so many other things."

Cangjie wakes up to the first birdcalls outside his window. The sky is bluing. He walks along the hawthorn path to the woods. The sun rises above the horizon, erasing darkness in the trees while casting shadows along the way.

At the entrance, instead of his mother he has half expected to see, two hunters are studying tracks in the trails. "I'm hunting deer today," one says, gazing at a row of hoofprints shaped like stretched, upside-down hearts. "I'm hunting fox," the other says, pointing at the tracks on the other trail, each featuring four toes, four claws, and a triangular heel pad.

Every animal leaves a unique imprint on the earth, Cangjie thinks. With one look at its tracks, the image of the whole animal jumps into the hunter's mind. Isn't that what his mother guided him to see? An imprint of a thing that projects the thing in the viewer's mind, the imprint unique and easy to draw with simple lines. But does every-thing leave an imprint somewhere? The sun, the moon, the mountains and rivers, where do they leave theirs? In the air, the sky, the eyes, the head that reads what the eyes see?

He heads home. His neighbor's children are out in the yard drawing with sticks.

The toddler draws a dot and a circle around it.

"What's this?" Cangjie asks.

"The sun."

They both look at the sun that has now risen above the canopy.

"What is the sun?" Cangjie asks.

"It's round and it shines," the boy says.

"I'm drawing a baby," says their younger daughter, three or four years old.

He sees a figure with a large head and two arms branching out of a line curving leftwards.

"With one leg?"

"No, that's his swaddling cloth. He can't walk on his own yet."

"I'm drawing a bird flying," says their older daughter, five or six.

There, etched in the dirt, is a pair of wings layered on top of each other.

Cangjie goes home, picks up the turtle shell and knife by his bed, and carves the following signs:

⊙ 𝕻 𝕵

They stand for *sun*, *baby*, and *flying* or *to fly*. The first sign is an exact copy of the toddler's drawing. The other two are simplified versions of the siblings'.

Then he carves more signs—𝕵 for *moon*, 𝖶 for *mountain*, 𝕭 for *tree*, and 𝕺 for *eye* or *to see*.

He goes to the court and shows the seven signs to the Yellow Emperor, who strokes his long silver beard and nods.

·

Cangjie starts to go about the villages and markets, collecting people's drawings, scribbles, and marks that are used for trade or personal symbols. When he sees images that fit what they stand for, he distills them and carves them onto a turtle shell, an ox bone, a bamboo slat, or a piece of tree bark. He has come to accept that there are no pure or full signifiers: only approximations, and compromise is an inevitable part of his task. But each time he carves a sign, he feels a flicker of solace, as though he has momentarily stilled something fleeting through the air, as though he has added another stroke in his re-creation of his mother's face, the world's face.

"What's water?" he asks an old woman washing clothes by the river.

"It's moving and it doesn't stay still," the woman says, looking into the water.

He draws a wavy line in the dirt. "Is this water?"

"No, it's a snake."

He draws two wavy lines. "Is this better?"

"No, it's a winding path."

He looks at the water fluttering in the river and draws again. "How about this?"

The woman nods. And Cangjie carves 川 for *water* on his turtle shell.

"What are stars?" he asks an old man sitting on a stump, chewing tea leaves with his bare gums.

The old man looks up. "They're shiny pebbles in the sky."

"Where are they from?"

"From nothing,"

"Nothing," Cangjie mumbles to himself. "What's nothing?"

"The other side of something," the old man says. "Think of a plant. It wasn't there on the earth, then came a seed, and it's there."

Cangjie thinks awhile, carves by the moonlight a plant sprouting out of the earth and a series of circles around it: 🪴 . "What do you think?"

The old man squints at the image. "It will do."

·

Alone at home, Cangjie continues to make signs by candlelight. What about feelings? How to draw them? He remembers a public execution when he was a child. A prisoner was tied to a beam in the town square, his upper body stripped, his heart thrashing beneath his shallow ribcage like a netted fish. A man in a black hood carved a bleeding circle around it with the tip of his knife. Cangjie's mother pressed his face to her belly and covered his ears with her hands, but of course he saw it—the torn-out heart still beating, stunned by its sudden eviction, the dark blood dripping thick and fast. He felt his own heart stop beating for a long second, as blankness seized him.

Cangjie carves 忄 on a bamboo slat for *heart*. He carves 忄日 for *terror*—a heart and a sudden blankness; 䰟 for *remembrance*—the head and the heart connected and facing the same direction; 恩 for *gratitude*—a person encircled by a larger pair of arms and feeling cared for, protected.

In dreams, his mother appears in the same way—sitting on her heels at the entrance of the woods, as if waiting. She looks like an old tree, blind and wise. If you put your hand on her wrinkled skin, your pain will drain toward her.

He carves 夢 for *dream*—a man lying on a bed with eyes closed but who still sees, sees more clearly than while awake.

·

As the Yellow Emperor commands, Cangjie teaches the signs to the representatives from the kingdom's nine provinces. During the lessons, he will sometimes forget what a sign means: 行, for example—does it mean *crossroads* or *lost* or *travel*? He tries to remember the day he made the sign. It was an iron-blue day and the first snow had just started to fall when he came to an empty crossroads. He stopped and looked up at the flakes falling toward the earth without a sound. When he lowered his face, he suddenly did not know which way he was going.

"This sign," he says to the staring representatives, "means 'travel if you know the way.'"

Oftentimes during the lessons, he recognizes how insufficient a sign is. 女 , for example, refers to "woman" and depicts a figure with protruding chest sitting on her heels. But women do not just sit on their heels sewing or nursing. His mother had worked in the field carrying him on her back, had chased away bullies and dogs. A woman cannot be reduced to this one posture that resembles kneeling. But it is in this posture that women are often seen, and it is in this posture that his mother appears in his dreams.

•

Before his death, Cangjie collects and creates five thousand signs. Since then, many of them have changed shape and picked up new referents. Some have lost their referents, left dangling and indecipherable. No one knows which is the last sign he carves before he closes his four eyes for good. Maybe it is ∩ , tying a knot at each end of a rope, which he used to do to signify the end of an event or the last season of a year, before he set out to find the world a parallel existence, a portable one.

Or maybe it is ◉ , the spiral he sees on snail shells and has been seeing everywhere during the last days of his life—in his fingerprints, in children's eyes, in the wind, the river, the sky. It stands for something that he cannot grasp, something that begins where there is no beginning and ends where there is no end.

Or maybe his last word is 好, a woman holding a child—his kneeling mother holding him on the roadside begging for food. The sign connotes so much to him that he cannot pin it down to one or two definitions. It can be a verb, a noun, an adjective, an adverb. It's an image he continues to see when he closes his eyes. In this waking dream, he walks down the winding path lined with hawthorn hedges to the poplar woods. His mother sits on her heels at the entrance. He walks to her and helps her up.

ACKNOWLEDGMENTS

My immense gratitude to Caroline Eisenmann and Megha Majumdar for their editorial acuity, their commitment and care.

Thanks to the superb team at Catapult, to the National Endowment for the Arts and the Sustainable Arts Foundation; to Judy Yung and Benson Tong's scholarship on early Chinese immigrants in America; Debra E. Meyerson and Danny Zuckerman's *Identity Theft: Rediscovering Ourselves After Stroke*; Peter Hessler's *Oracle Bones*; the documentaries *Disturbing the Peace* by Ai Weiwei, *Who Killed Our Children* by Pan Jianlin, and *Our Children* by Ai Xiaoming; and to the editors of 《象形字典》, where I learned about many of the Oracle Bone signs in the collection.

Thanks to Michael Nelson for his insightful comments on the early drafts of the stories, and to early readers Trudy Lewis, E. C. Osondu, and Naira Kuzmich.

Thanks to Rachel Michelle Hanson, He Jiawei, Paul B.

Roth, Mary Alice Mills, Jess Camara, Fumiko Yasuhara, Akio Yasuhara, Lisa Russ Spaar, D. A. Powell, Jane Lunin Perel, Chard deNoid, Peggy Reid, Speer Morgan, Christopher Nelson, Carolyn Forché, Ann Marie Long, and Kevin Stamp for their friendship and support.

I am grateful to my grandmothers, Zhang Yuhua and Li Xuefeng, whose voices I seek to listen to with this writing; to my aunt, Ye Xiufeng, for her compassion and resilience; to my mother and father, Kang Rongfen and Ye Yuwei, and my sister, Ye Qing, for always being there for me; and to Shawn and Mira Feifei, without whom this book could not exist.

© Mira Feifei Ye-Flanagan

YE CHUN is a bilingual Chinese American writer and literary translator. She has published two books of poetry, *Travel Over Water* and *Lantern Puzzle*; a novel in Chinese, 《海上的桃树》 (Peach Tree in the Sea); and four volumes of translations. A recipient of an NEA Literature Fellowship, a Sustainable Arts Foundation Award, and three Pushcart Prizes, she teaches at Providence College and lives in Providence, Rhode Island.